The Earth is Singing

"What would I want from you, you dirty Jew?" Marija says. "I want the same as everybody else in here. To get you out of our country."

I am so shocked that for a moment the room spins and I think, I can't have heard that right.

Dirty Jew.

Dirty Jew.

Dirty Jew.

"I was born in Rīga, same as you," I say. "I'm Latvian, just like you."

In answer, Marija spits a warm gob of phlegm right into my face.

USBORNE MODERN CLASSICS

Introducing timeless stories to today's readers

VANESSA CURTIS

The Earth is Singing

USBORNE MODERN CLASSICS

Dedicated to Ita Edie Michalowitz, 1882 - 1957

This edition first published in the UK in 2019 by Usborne Publishing Ltd., Usborne House, 83-85 Saffron Hill, London EC1N 8RT, England. www.usborne.com

A CIP catalogue record for this book is available from the British Library.

ISBN 9781474958660 03230/7 JFMAMJJASON /18

Printed in UK.

Author's Note

My great-grandmother was born in Talsi, a tiny village outside Rīga, the capital of Latvia, at a time when Latvia was part of the Russian Empire. After the bloody upheaval of the 1905 Russian Revolution, she left Latvia and arrived by ship at the East London Docks to start a safer life. But I got to wondering what had happened to the relatives she left behind in Rīga and my research revealed the unbearable truth. They were Jews, so their fate during World War II was to be the worst imaginable.

Latvia left the Russian Empire and was an independent country from 1920 to 1940. But in 1940, towards the beginning of World War II, the Soviet army again occupied Latvia, under the pretext of protecting it from the Germans. They installed a Communist government.

Latvia became part of the Soviet Union and was once more governed from Moscow.

The new Communist regime in Latvia was harsh. During the period of the Soviet dictator, Stalin, Latvians who were judged to be enemies of the State were tortured and interrogated on the sixth floor of the KGB building in Rīga and executed in the basement or the yard. Thousands more were sent to hard labour camps in Siberia. In June 1941, 15,500 Latvian residents, mostly from Rīga, including 5,000 Jews and some 2,400 children under ten, were arrested and deported to these labour camps by cattle truck.

Under Communist rule, factories, banks and private businesses were nationalized. Latvia's armed forces were destroyed. Organizations such as the Girl Guides and Boy Scouts were abolished, as well as all independent social organizations. All Latvian schoolchildren were forced to learn Russian as their first language in school and take part in Communist demonstrations. Churches, synagogues and other places of worship were shut down or repressed. Writers, musicians and artists were only allowed to produce works in accordance with Communist ideology. Any books which did not follow this ideology were banned from schools, libraries and bookshops and their creators were shot or sent to labour camps.

But worse was to come. The year of Soviet occupation in Latvia came to an abrupt end in July 1941 when Hitler's German army invaded. Many Latvians at first viewed the German army as saviours who would rescue them from the daily restrictions of that harsh Soviet Communist regime. There was even hope that Latvia's independence would be restored. But, for Rīga's 30,000 Jewish residents, any hopes were short-lived. Along with the German army came Adolf Hitler's vehemently anti-Semitic Nazi Party. The Nazis had only one plan for the Jews of Rīga – to wipe them out.

As the Soviet army retreated and the German army invaded, there was mass bombing and shelling in Rīga. The spire of St Peter's Church in the old town, a national monument since 1209, was caught by artillery fire and burned to the ground. As St Peter's burned, the Nazis began to put their dreadful plan into effect.

This is the story of what happened next.

Chapter One

29th June 1941, Rīga, Latvia

IT STARTS WITH THE NIGHT that St Peter's is bombed.

Mama stands behind me with her arms wrapped tight around my shoulders.

We watch from our apartment at the end of *Skārņu iela* as the church spire crumples like a giant bird's wing on fire and folds in slow motion to the ground.

It is hard to believe what is happening to the church. It has been there for hundreds of years.

Since Papa was taken, she has to hold me tight enough for him as well.

There is a deafening roar of collapsing rubble.

"It might be a last-ditch attempt by the Soviets," says Mama. "Or it might be a warning from the Germans. I hear they are on the other side of the riverbank already.

If they can destroy St Peter's, they can destroy anything."

"What do you mean?" I say. Mama has been saying a lot of things like this lately. Sometimes I understand them and sometimes it's as if she has stopped speaking German and started in some other language.

Mama pulls the curtains and shuts out the orange flames and thick grey plumes of smoke rising from the bomb site. The city has been under fire for several weeks now. We are getting used to only venturing out if we really have to. Mama is annoyed that she can't visit the Central Market to buy meat to make our weekly Sabbath meal, but it's just too dangerous to walk that far. Instead she queues with other housewives at the small kosher butcher on the corner of our street and comes home disgruntled with overpriced, fatty meat.

"The Germans," says Mama. "They are announcing their intent. It's a sign to us."

I sigh. My mother can be very melodramatic.

"Perhaps they will make things better," I say. "I mean – how can things get much worse after what has happened to Papa?"

My mother turns away and goes into the tiny kitchen at the back of our apartment. I can hear her chopping liver with a small sharp knife. Liver is one of the few things still in ready supply and my mother serves it up every

Sabbath and most weekday nights. In the two weeks since Papa left, her Jewish faith seems to have deepened. She says it's for the sake of Omama, my grandmother, but I reckon it's giving her something to be busy with so she doesn't have to think about what's happened to us.

The knife echoes on the chopping board like the snap of bones.

I go and look out of the window again. Nobody will try to extinguish the flames. The Russians have torched as many buildings as possible on their exit from our town. Rīga has been burning and smouldering for what seems like for ever. Vecrīga – the old town – is littered with the shells of buildings. They have large gaping windows and roofs which are open to the sky. The gutters are full of ash and debris and you can see bullet holes in the walls of some of the ornate art nouveau houses. Their bright yellow and blue facades look like they've been infected with chickenpox.

If I strain my head to the right I can still see the chimneys of Papa's factory and the gothic roof of our old villa.

My stomach aches with pain. Mama has told me that the Russians need Papa for something overseas. Since they invaded us last year they have taken over control of banks and factories and started to view many Latvians as enemies of the state. That's why they stole Papa's factory, stopped him making a living for his family and then came to our villa in the middle of the night and made him throw two shirts and a pair of trousers and a few cooking pots into a bag. He left under cover of darkness. Somebody in town said that the men and women had been separated at the railway station and then shoved into cattle trucks. That's why when I think about the 14th June, my heart aches. I try not to think about Papa in his elegant suit and white shirt being shoved into a truck. He is always so smart and takes pride in his appearance. I can't bear to think of him suffering in any way at all. My papa is a good man.

The Soviets told us we no longer owned our villa, either.

We were ordered to move into this small apartment on *Skārņu iela* and even though it is in a solid old building and on a pretty street, it's not our home.

Mama is fearful of the German soldiers heading towards Rīga but I don't know why. They can hardly make things worse for us than the Soviets have.

"Mama," I say, going into the kitchen. "I thought you loved everything German. You are always telling me that they are a cultured race. You speak their language and you love their buildings. Why are you so scared?"

My mother is spooning pickles from a jar into a small

brown bowl. She puts it down and comes over to where I'm leaning on the door frame.

"Hanna," she says, "it is not so simple. I don't want to scare you, but haven't you noticed the reaction we're getting in the streets?"

"Yes, a little," I say. I am cleaning the soft pink leather of my ballet shoes ready for dance school on Monday. I have noticed some strange glances from some of the girls at school and I've been worrying over whether to say something to them or just try and ignore it.

I used to go to a Jewish school and speak Hebrew, but when the Soviets invaded us just over a year ago they forced all the schoolchildren in Latvia, regardless of their religion, to go to regular school and learn Russian as a first language. I didn't want that, so I auditioned for the School of the Opera and Ballet Theatre of LSSR instead and have spent the past year of Soviet occupation doing dance full-time. I liked the fact that I was allowed to do this; to follow my dreams of dancing like a swan.

But that was before they took Papa and changed our lives for ever.

I'm about to ask Mama more questions because I feel like she's hiding something from me, but our plan to sit down to an early supper is disrupted by a knock on the door.

I go to open it and my face breaks into a grin.

"You found us!"

I hold open the door and invite him in.

Uldis Lapa is my best friend.

And maybe a little more.

I think I have loved Uldis for as long as I can remember. And now I think he is starting to feel the same way. We have been friends since I was ten and have been going out to the cinema together since I was fourteen.

He also taught me to swim at the big Rīga baths in town. But I always wanted to be more than just his best friend. So when I turned fifteen I asked Mama if, instead of going swimming or to see a film, I could take a special picnic to the park and sit by the canal with Uldis. I wanted to tell him how I felt.

We sat by the big white Opera House where I have dreams of dancing onstage one day and I opened up the picnic hamper and displayed all the good things that Mama had made me: black bread, sour cream, cold sausages, smoked sprats and a bottle of lemonade to wash it all down.

Uldis ate with enthusiasm. He always does. And I didn't eat much because I had a feeling he was going to turn to me and offer a proper kiss and I didn't want my memory of that day to be of my embarrassment at stinking of fish.

When Uldis had gulped down the dregs of his lemonade he wiped his mouth on one of Mama's best linen napkins and then he leaned in towards me. There was a slight breeze and it lifted his blond peak of hair so that his bright blue eyes seemed even brighter against the tan of his skin.

And then he kissed me.

Something changed from that moment onwards. We stopped larking about and teasing one another like we'd done since I was a child and Uldis reached out for my hand as we crossed the little bridge in the park and leaned over towards the water.

I looked down at his quivering reflection in the water and my own, shorter one next to it and I thought: *I might marry you one day, Uldis Lapa.*

Uldis still lives next door to our old villa, with his parents and sister. We were told not to tell our neighbours where we were being moved to, but I missed Uldis so much for the first few days, and deep down I just knew that he'd do everything he could to find me.

He is seventeen and has just left school to do an apprenticeship at one of the lawyers' offices in the centre of town. He is a bright boy, or so Papa was always telling me. I think that Papa hoped I'd marry Uldis one day. But Mama always developed her tight-lipped look whenever Papa spoke that way. Sometimes I wonder if it's because she would like me to make a Jewish marriage. But the thing is, that Mama didn't make one either.

Today, though, she's not looking tight-lipped at all. Just weary, and unsurprised to see Uldis standing on our front doorstep like an eager puppy, clutching a bunch of wilted flowers and a bottle of Rīga Black Balsam. My mother hates the stuff, but Omama loves it.

It's been two weeks since Omama moved in with us. As soon as Papa went, she promised to help my mother look after me. She's Mama's mother and very devout in her Judaism. I've been dragged twice to the *Peitav Shul* since she came to live with us. Before that we never used to bother very much with attending synagogue because although Mama is Jewish, Papa isn't. He's Latvian, born here in Rīga and he speaks fluent Latvian, unlike Mama and Omama whose ancestors came from a German-speaking part of Latvia.

She is out of her rocking chair and hobbling towards the door. She grabs the bottle from Uldis, gives him a searching look and limps back to the chair. Within seconds she's quaffing the black liquid out of a sizeable glass.

Rīgans swear by the power of Black Balsam. It's made up of vodka and various plant extracts. I tasted it once and nearly died. But Omama uses it for everything – colds, coughs and cuts. She even uses it to clean the bath and disinfect the lavatory although that's not what the manufacturers recommend.

That's my crazy Omama for you.

Omama is old, but she's not nearly as feeble as she makes out. She likes to give the impression of a mad old Jewish grandmother in a black headscarf, muttering and rocking in her chair and stuffing her face with gefilte fish balls and smoked salmon, but her eyes in her wrinkled face are so bright that they're at odds with the rest of her appearance.

Omama likes Uldis. She would prefer that he was Jewish but he gets round that by bringing her food and drink and having nice manners. Besides, she knows full well that I've got no intention of marrying anybody for a good while yet.

I'm planning on staying at my ballet school for the six years it takes to train to be a professional dancer. It's what I have always wanted to do. Mama has told me that I should do science or maths but even she can't deny the fact that I move like a swan, and swans need to keep swimming.

I also love music. I sing all the time. I feel like singing

now, because my dear Uldis has found me and is hovering on the doorstep with an impish grin on his face.

Mama beckons him to come inside and shut the door.

"We have plenty of food," she says to Uldis. She is speaking Latvian as that is Uldis's first language. It sounds unfamiliar coming from her mouth. "Come and join us."

Uldis kisses my cheek, blushing a little. Our relationship still feels very new and raw. Everything is exaggerated in intensity. The slightest look from him can leave me feeling naked and vulnerable, as if the whole world can see how I'm feeling without me even having to say a word.

Omama is already at the table, piling up a plate with eggs, cheeses and pickles.

I cut slices of dark Latvian bread. Even my arm cutting the bread feels all shaky under Uldis's intense gaze, and a few nuts and seeds fall out onto the bread board. Omama is always telling me that this bread is a lifesaver if you get a fishbone stuck in your throat. Something about the density of the bread just frightens that bone right down your gullet.

Omama likes the caraway variety, so that's why my mother always gets it. Sometimes she bakes her own, but it's a time-consuming business and can make her bad-tempered.

There's not so much time to waste now that Papa's factory has been taken over by the Soviets. Mama has expanded her sewing business and is often up all night, hunched over her machine, foot pounding up and down with a bang. The banging is right next to my bedroom, but I daren't complain. If Mama can't work, we will end up on the streets.

Uldis sits at the small table at the end of our living room where we've tried to make a tiny dining area. He eats with relish, surveying the food on his plate with pleasure. It gives me a chance to look at him without being observed.

He's tall, with fair hair that sweeps to one side over clear blue eyes and a healthy complexion from all the swimming and sports that he does outside of his apprenticeship. Sometimes I think that we look a lot alike. I don't look Jewish, unlike Mama who has very dark brown hair and olive skin and what Papa refers to as a "distinguished" nose. I look more like Papa, who has the fair look of many Latvians. My hair falls in a light-brown plait down my back and my skin flushes easily. I too have got blue eyes, but mine are darker, almost navy.

"How is your work progressing?" Mama is asking Uldis. "How many years until you qualify to work as a lawyer?"

Uldis pauses for a second, with a gherkin frozen midway to his mouth.

"Uh – I'm not sure," he says. "I heard that the Latvian police are hoping to recruit volunteers to aid the German army in Rīga. I might try out for that."

Omama drops her knife and fork with an indignant clatter.

"A policeman?" she says. "What do you need to fight for? You already live on Latvian soil. You have a good life and the prospect of an excellent career."

I glance at Mama. She has gone very pale underneath her dark skin. She picks at a pile of pickles and then goes into the kitchen to get the cheesecake she baked earlier. When she comes back her colour has changed and her face looks flushed, as if she has a fever coming.

"But Uldis," she begins, "surely you know what the Germans will be doing when they get here? You don't wish to be part of that! Have you not heard the rumours from Poland?"

We have all heard the rumours. It has been said from late last year that the Polish Jews have been forced to leave their homes and herded into some sort of ghetto area in Warsaw. But nobody is sure and it seems so hard to believe that this could happen to ordinary people that I try to convince Mama that rumours are not always true.

Uldis gulps his cheesecake and pushes back his chair.

"I just came to check you were all okay," he says, with a big smile at Mama. "Thanks for the food, Mrs Michelson."

My mother does not smile back.

I show Uldis out.

"Sorry about that," I say. I look up at his tall frame. "It's so good to see you. When will I see you again?"

Uldis is putting on his jacket. Summer in Rīga can feel like March. There's an ice-cold wind which whips through the Baltics at this time of year.

He looks down at me. There's something in his eyes that I can't read. If I had to try, I'd say it had a slightly sad quality. But that can't be right, because then he turns to me and gives me his wide smile and says: "Perhaps we could go swimming next week? I will pick you up on Saturday morning."

He leans over me and kisses the top of my head. Electric thrills shoot right through my body to my feet.

Then he leaves me standing there. I watch him bolt downstairs.

On the last day of June I'm awake at one o'clock in the morning.

Outside comes something I haven't heard for a long time.

Silence.

The last Russian tanks have finally rolled out of town, leaving destruction and ruin in their wake. The dust from the tracks of the tank wheels has hardly settled. St Peter's church smoulders gently at the end of *Skārņu iela*, a strange spire-less structure that bears no resemblance to a holy place any longer. Behind the stump I can now see the four giant arches of the old Zeppelin hangars which house our beloved Central Market.

It's too quiet. I can't sleep.

I get out of my camp bed and pull back the curtains.

The lack of noise is so heavy that it makes my ears ache and strain. All I can hear is that eerie silence. It feels loaded with something that is yet to happen. The feeling reminds me of being little and putting a cup filled with water on top of a door, hiding behind it and waiting for Papa to open the door and get a soaking.

I've got used to hearing the sounds of police sirens and fire engines. I've almost got used to the sounds of shooting and shelling, bombing and screaming.

But on this night there is nothing. Nothing.

I hug my elbows and hum an old Jewish nursery rhyme to fill the silence.

Under baby's cradle in the night
Stands a goat so soft and snowy white
The goat will go to the market
To bring you wonderful treats
He'll bring you raisins and almonds
Sleep, my little one, sleep.

I gaze out over the roofs and spires of the city I love. There are gaps and holes but it is still my beloved Rīga.

The silence does not last for long.

Chapter Two

When I wake up the next day there's another unfamiliar sound coming from the streets.

Singing.

I stick my head out of the window. The pavements outside are crowded with people, jostling and talking. There are speakers in the middle of the street, blasting out our Latvian national anthem.

"Merciful God, can't an old woman sleep in?" Omama is muttering in her tiny bedroom, but she too is leaning her bony elbows on the window sill and staring down at the scenes outside.

"I haven't heard that since before the Soviets came," says Mama, laying up plates and bowls for our breakfast. "If only I could believe that all the trouble was over."

"Maybe it is," I say. "There are people carrying flowers and greeting the soldiers, Mama. Look!"

I stare down at the German army, men who are supposed to be our saviours and free us from the Soviet regime. They have thick brown arms in tight khaki uniforms and hats which look like helmets. They are armed with brown guns and their faces are exhausted but cheerful. There are Latvian women in traditional white peasant dress running out of the crowd to kiss them and offer them flowers.

"Nothing could be worse than what has happened to us already," I say in what I hope is a firm voice. "What could be worse than Papa being taken away?"

I seem to smell Papa when I mention his name. Often that faint whiff of the aftershave he always wore when he was about to go to a business meeting or out on a date with Mama. The smell is painful and comforting all at the same time.

Omama heaves herself into the chair next to me and pinches my cheek so hard that my eyes water. It's her way of showing affection, but I wish she wouldn't.

"Your papa will come back one day soon," she says. "Now that the Soviets have gone, they will perhaps release him."

Mama lets out a dramatic sigh and flips her tea cloth impatiently at both of us.

"Eat your breakfast and stop speculating," she says. "Hanna, you need to get to dance school."

She ignores my pout of protest. There's far too much going on outside for me to want to miss it all.

"And, Mama," she says under her breath to her own mother, "stop giving the girl false hopes. She knows as well as I do what the rumours are. And you know that they hold us responsible for everything that has happened."

Those rumours again. They are so terrifying that I try to shut them out in my mind with a thick curtain of black. They can't affect us here in Rīga. After all, this is not Poland. We are different in almost every way. Our language, our food, our history are all different. It is only our religion that we have in common with the Jews of Poland.

"I have heard the rumours," I say to Mama, "but still I don't understand what we have actually done wrong."

I am hoping that Mama is about to tell me.

But she just eats her bread with a closed-off look on her face.

I drag myself to school, dawdling as much as I can. I push my way through the cheering crowds and listen to the sound of the German soldiers' feet as they march through the city centre. All the way to my school there are people lining the streets, waving flags and flowers and kissing one another as if at last they are free.

I cut past the beautiful white *Opera* in the park and stop to stare at it. The building is a little like a garlanded white wedding cake to look at, surrounded by the bright pink and orange flowers of the park and the gentle canal with the little bridge over it.

One day I plan to dance here. Mama will be in the audience with Papa and Omama, who will probably still be alive even if she's over a hundred by then. I will stand on the stage and spin and pirouette and jeté in a white costume studded with silver and I will dance the dance of Rīga and its spire-studded beauty. I will dance of love and life and all the possibilities which it has.

Papa always taught me to grab life with both hands.

The night before he was taken away, he called me into the spacious wood-panelled study that we had in the villa. "My little dancing daughter," he said, his eyes filling with water. "My little songbird." The room reeked of pipe smoke but I didn't mind. "Promise me", he said, "you will always try to live. Whatever happens. Keep living. And look after Mama. Promise me?"

I laughed at the time. I thought that Papa was being overemotional and silly. I liked him calling me "little dancing daughter" because it made me feel special and cherished.

"Sure, Papa," I said. Then I skipped off back to my bedroom.

It was only later that the thought struck me like a ton of rubble.

Papa spoke as if he knew he was to be taken away.

And the very next day, he was.

When I reach the *Brīvības bulvāris* where the *Brīvības piemineklis*, our Freedom Monument, is located, the sheer number of people there takes my breath away.

I stop and stare up. The monument is forty-two metres high. I've had that fact drummed into me at school for as long as I can remember. It was put up after the Latvian War of Independence to commemorate soldiers who died, but ever since then people have congregated here whenever anything of national importance has happened. There are flowers laid at the foot of the monument every single day and there are always at least two armed guards standing motionless in front of it. When I was a little girl I was very worried about how the guards would fare if they needed the lavatory, but Mama said that they worked in shifts and that every hour a new guard would take over.

At the top of the column is a statue of Liberty carrying three gilded stars over her head.

Everybody is looking up at the top of the statue today, like they're seeing it in a new light.

I push my way towards the monument because I need to get to my school on the other side of town. It's not easy. I smell the sweat of unwashed bodies and sickly-sweet blooms as I elbow my way past the soldiers and the over-excited Latvian women who are darting out to press their flowers upon the German soldiers on horseback. It is a rare hot day, with sunshine beating down on the stones of the *bulvāris* and the old people already huddled under the shady trees in the park.

I get to the other side of the monument, panting for breath.

And it is then that I see something odd.

There is a column of young men with their heads hanging low, being marched off towards the outskirts of the old town by a group of soldiers.

The soldiers are not wearing the uniforms of the German army. They have red and white armbands on a khaki uniform and are clutching guns.

The guns are pointing at the heads of the young men.

My arms chill with cold.

I stare at the column of men again. One or two of

them look familiar. I realize with a jolt of horror that I can see some of the boys who used to be a couple of years above me at my last school. They can be no more than seventeen or eighteen years old.

But where are they going?

I watch them being marched off. If other people have seen, they are choosing not to comment. Most of them are still facing the other way, cheering at the soldiers' parade.

I wait until the young men have been marched round a corner and out of sight and then I run back through the crowds and in the direction of home.

I have to tell Mama.

Mama is not too pleased that I've skipped dance school.

"Hanna, I've got work to do," she says, pointing at the mountain of fabric in front of her on the table. We don't have Mama's sewing table any longer, although we managed to sneak her machine out of the villa. So the dining-room table doubles up as a work table after I have gone to school.

"Where's Omama?" I say. She's usually snoring in her chair or shelling peas whilst moaning about something or other.

"She wanted to go out and see what was happening," says Mama. "I told her to be careful. The streets are not really the place for a frail old woman."

She catches my eye and we both break out laughing. There's nothing frail about Omama, as we both know.

My smile fades.

"I need to tell you something," I say.

Mama passes me the bagel I forgot to eat at breakfast time. I smear it with cream cheese and smoked salmon and gulp it down. Mama is very pretty, which helps with buying food. Papa always said that she could charm the birds out of the trees, but we don't have too many trees around here and the birds have been scared off by the bombing and continual fires.

"I just saw a group of young men being marched away from the Freedom Monument," I say.

"Yes?" says Mama. "Soviet prisoners of war, I expect."

"No," I say. "They were not Soviets. They were just boys. And the soldiers were not in German uniforms. They had red armbands."

Omama has come in while we are talking. She is regarding me with her bright brown eyes. She is eating pickles with greed, scooping them up and shoving them into her mouth, which is half-open with her two front false teeth on show.

"That is the new Latvia police," she says. "Your Uldis has designs on becoming one of those."

I am so surprised that a laugh bursts out of me.

"Uldis is a good person," I say. "He would never hurt people."

I think back to last year. I was in the park with Uldis and a bee flew straight into the top of my ice-cream cone. He spent ages trying to coax it onto a leaf and then put it in the sun so that it could dry out its wings. Together we watched the tiny insect struggle back to life and dart away.

"Did you recognize any of the young men?" Mama says. "Perhaps they were in training to become soldiers."

I picture the group of men in my mind. I see their hanging heads and the look of shame and fear on some of their faces.

I see the muzzle of the guns shoved into the small of the young men's backs and for a dizzy moment I actually have a flash of what it must have felt like.

"Yes," I say. "I recognized some of them from school."

Mama and Omama exchange looks.

"Dance school?" says Mama.

I sigh and reach for another bagel.

"No," I say. "Ezra."

Ezra was the school I used to go to, before the Soviets invaded us.

"Jews?" says Omama, still chewing. Her eyes never leave my face.

"I guess so," I say. I had been so shocked by the guns in their backs that it had taken me a little while to realize this.

"Where were they going?" says Mama. Her cheeks are bright pink. "Did you see?"

"Mm," I say, my mouth full of fish and cheese. "*Aspazijas bulvāris.*"

"My God," says Mama.

"Ah," says Omama. "They were being taken to the prefecture."

Mama darts Omama a furious glance and flaps her hands to quieten her but it's too late. Now I want to know.

I wait until Mama begins to prepare lunch for later.

Then I whisper, "Omama – what is happening in the prefecture? Is it bad?" The prefecture is our police station.

My grandmother fidgets about in the pocket of the black dress she always wears and produces a squashed caramel in a faded gold wrapper.

"I'm not ten," I protest, but she forces me to take it before hobbling over to the chair in the corner for her nap.

Within seconds she is snoring, her head dropped on one side.

Mama comes in with a new pile of fabric and we spend the rest of the morning cutting and sewing to the endless sounds of cheering and marching outside. Or at least, Mama sews and I cut.

The Latvian national anthem is played on and off all day along with another song I don't recognize. This second song is rigid in time and sounds very patriotic. I ask Mama what it is and she snaps off a length of thread with her teeth and doesn't answer for a moment.

"It is the anthem of the Nazi Party," she says when I continue to stare at her.

"Oh," I say. A tiny bolt of something painful passes through my stomach. "They are already here, then?"

"Yes," says Mama. She doesn't elaborate.

My mind is racing.

I keep replaying in my head the expressions on the faces of those young Jewish men as they were marched off.

I see the red and white armbands on the uniforms of the men accompanying them.

Uldis might be wearing those armbands soon. What if he is ordered to stick a gun into the back of a thin Jewish boy?

But I know him so well. He is kind. He won't harm anyone. He will keep the peace.

I want to discuss it with Mama, but something about

her face is as closed off as the sign outside our famous church warning people not to venture inside the ruin.

So the questions and doubts inside me have nowhere to go.

They grow into the silence, filling it up like mould.

Chapter Three

Mrs Rubinstein and her family are taken away in the night.

I wake up from an uneasy sleep to hear screaming.

Mama is already up and standing in her red flannel dressing gown at the window, her hair in a dark plait down her back. For the first time I notice the wiry grey hairs poking out and floating in the lamplight.

I stand next to her and we peer out of the gap in the curtains. Mama tells me to switch off the light.

Down on the street the white-clad figure of Mrs Rubinstein, still in a nightdress, can be seen huddled over next to a man in sharp uniform with a smart peaked cap to match. Her two children cling to her hands. I can hear little Peter crying and see his older sister, Leah, trying to comfort him. She is crouched down, peering into his face.

I stare at the soldier. He looks different to the ones who marched through Rīga with their wide grins and tanned faces.

I can't see much of his face because it's dark, but something about the rigid way he holds himself makes my stomach feel horrid. He is pencil-thin and full of sharp angles.

"Why are they taking her?" I whisper, almost to myself as much as to Mama.

Mama doesn't answer. Mrs Rubinstein was our neighbour when we lived in the villa and she was moved at the same time we were, to the apartment block right next door to ours. Now she is being shoved into the back of a truck. As she sits in her thin nightdress, she looks up at our apartment for a split second and Mama places the palm of her hand on the window and it's like a message passes between them via electricity.

We watch as the truck with the three figures in the back passes down our street and roars out of sight.

There is a terrible silence for about five minutes. The truck drives off so fast that I can still see leaves and debris swirling around on the pavement. Mama pulls her long coat over her nightdress and runs downstairs and out into the street. I see her bend over something in the gutter. When she comes back upstairs she is sighing heavily and I don't think it's from her exertions on the staircase.

She puts something on the window sill in front of us.

It's the dirty stuffed teddy bear belonging to Peter Rubinstein. It only has one black beaded eye.

"We will keep it until he gets back," says Mama, her eyes shining. "I will sew on a new eye and give this bear back his sight!"

I smile. Sometimes Mama can be strict and hard to fathom.

At other times I love her so much that it hurts.

The silence outside doesn't last long. The sound of screams and gunfire reach us from somewhere just around the corner – *Kalēju iela*, perhaps.

Mama makes us a cup of coffee each as it's obvious that we will not be able to sleep any longer that night. Already I know that I will fail to reach school in a few hours' time.

"Mama," I say, fiddling with the ends of my hair. "The Germans have chased the Soviets out of town but it does not feel safe. I can still hear shooting."

Omama has woken up and come in to see what we

are talking about. Mama pours her a cup of strong black coffee and gets out a tin of biscuits.

"Mama," I say, with more insistence in my voice this time. "Why did they take Mrs Rubinstein away?"

My mother looks like she is wrestling with something in her head. She plays for time by dipping a caraway biscuit into her coffee and chewing on it in a very deliberate way.

"Tell the girl, Kristina," says Omama. "She's not a baby any longer."

"Thank you," I say, indignant.

Mama gets up and looks out of the window again. Then she turns around and stands behind me with her hands on my shoulders.

"They are shooting Jews," she says. "And they have taken Mrs Rubinstein away because she too is a Jew."

She brushes my fringe off my forehead and rakes her fingers through my hair.

I nod. Mama is expecting me to be brave and understanding, so I try to look serious.

"Is there some other reason, though?" I say. "I mean – has she done something wrong, other than just being a Jew?"

Mrs Rubinstein is a very gentle, nervous lady. We saw her nearly every day, outside supervising her children in the small back garden of the apartments or hustling them down the street to the kosher butcher's shop. She had the same large, dark worried eyes that could be seen on the faces of her children.

"Oh, Hanna," says Mama. She drinks the dregs of her coffee and sinks her head into her hands. "She has done nothing wrong. As you say – she is just a Jew."

"But you are a Jew," I say. I can hear my voice rising up a bit in panic. "So why didn't they take you? Or Omama?"

Omama snorts. I can almost hear her saying, "Pity the soldier who tries to take ME away. I'll hit him with my stick!"

"Because I am lucky this time," says Mama. "Because I pray every night to God that He will leave me here to look after you. Because I promised your father" – and here she swallows back tears – "that I would always protect you from harm."

I feel sick. I push my cup away and hang on to Mama's hand.

"First the Soviets hate us because we are proud to be Latvian," I say. "And now the Germans hate us because we are Jews. What have we ever done to them?"

Mama sighs.

"It is complex," she says. "But it is not all Germans

who hate the Jews. Just the Nazis. They are working for Hitler and *he* hates the Jews."

"Why?" I say. I know that my questions are wearing Mama out and Omama is flashing her eyes at me, which probably means that I should stop, but I can't seem to hold the words back. It's like a whole new section of my future life has just started up without me even wanting it to.

"He blames them," says Mama. She sounds so matter-of-fact, like she's discussing the Sabbath dinner menu.

"For what?" I say. "I promise that is my last question."

Mama gathers the cups and helps Omama from her chair. When she turns back to me her eyes have taken on a haunted expression I've never seen before. I can trace back her family and her family's family and even ancestors before that, in those pain-filled eyes.

"For everything," she says. "He blames the Jews for everything."

The next day is Friday.

I am not allowed to attend school, just as I had predicted. The streets are too dangerous.

Mama goes out on her own after breakfast to get the

ingredients she needs for the Sabbath dinner tonight and the meals we will have tomorrow. In the new paper, *Tēvija*, published every day in Rīga, there is an announcement for Jews. It says that we are banned from shopping anywhere that has a queue of people outside it. We are not supposed to mix with the rest of the population now.

Mama takes this piece of news with a shrug.

"We need to eat," she says. "I'm sure that our Latvian neighbours will turn a blind eye."

She ties a scarf over her head first and pulls on her shapeless coat and her stout brown lace-up shoes.

"I look like a good Latvian woman, no?" she says to her reflection in the mirror.

I stand upstairs at the window and watch her scurrying down *Skārņu iela*. She greets a couple of neighbours and acquaintances on the way but does not stop to chat.

At the corner of our street there is a soldier in a grey uniform with stiff boards on the shoulders and a cap with an eagle on the front. I stare. I have never seen such a uniform before.

Mama comes back half an hour later.

"There are queues everywhere," she says. "I had to join one. Mrs Karulis recognized me. But she didn't give me away. I kept my head down. There were other Jews like us in the queue, too."

"Like you," I correct her. I don't really count myself as Jewish. Papa wasn't, and I look a lot like him. If it wasn't for him being taken away, we wouldn't be observing so many Jewish rituals and festivals. We have always celebrated the Sabbath, though. Even Jews with no faith at all tend to sit down on a Friday night and hold the Sabbath meal. I am starting to wonder if this is a good thing. Already I feel as if I don't want to be at all connected with the Jews any longer. If Hitler is out to get them, then surely we should stop advertising our faith and try to blend in with the general population of Latvia?

I sigh. Mama would never agree to that. Her faith has become even more important since Papa went away. And Omama has the deepest faith of us all.

Mama is already preparing food in the kitchen. Because of our faith, Jews are not allowed to cook, bake or work after the Sabbath has formally begun, at eighteen minutes before sunset on a Friday night. Like nearly every Jewish woman we know, she prepares a cholent on Friday afternoon and leaves it to simmer overnight on a low heat in the oven, so that it will be ready for Saturday lunch the next day.

I loathe cholent. Omama says that's the whole point and that it's not supposed to taste all that nice as it has been eaten for hundreds of years by Jews who don't have a lot of money. It consists of a piece of slow-cooked, salty beef all stewed up with butter beans and potatoes.

I like the Sabbath supper on Friday nights much better.

Mama has already made two shiny loaves of challah – sweet, shiny bread wrapped into plaits a bit like my own. Her challah has three strands, which stand for truth, peace and justice. With the challah we will eat braised beef, fish in egg and lemon sauce, potato salad and potato kugel, my favourite thing. Kugel is a crispy pancake made of grated potato and fried until the inside is fluffy and soft. After this feast we will be served Mama's excellent sponge cake. It has no butter, which is just as well as Mama says that the shops are running out of it. But it is light and fluffy and made with lots of eggs.

By the time the food is prepared it is nearly sunset.

I am allowed to light the special candles. They are placed on our dining-room table, which has been laid with a white cloth and flowers and all Mama's best silver and china. The candles represent observance and remembrance.

Omama welcomes in the Sabbath queen by wafting her hands around the lit candles seven times. The queen represents a bride given to us by God. Then she says the blessing with her palms pressed over her eyes.

I like the comforting ritual of this blessing. Although I am not as religious as Omama, I know that God is up there looking after us all and keeping us safe.

Mama bows her head and I am sure she is thinking of Papa and wishing with all her heart that he might be allowed to come home again.

I close my eyes and wish it too. I wish it so hard that I forget to breathe and when I open my eyes I see stars.

I try not to peek at the challah sitting under the cloth that must cover them at the table until we are ready to break the bread.

I'm starving.

And we can't eat until Omama has taken herself off to the synagogue for forty-five minutes of prayer. She refuses point-blank to stay inside, even though Mama pleads with her and gestures to the noise coming from the streets outside.

"They will not harm me in the synagogue!" Omama says. "They would not dare touch such a holy place!"

She flaps her hands at Mama and puts on her long black coat and scarf. Then she hobbles off down six flights of stairs and emerges at the bottom panting for breath and leaning on the wall. Mama watches her until she has reached the end of our street and turned right towards the synagogue.

Then she sits back at the table and we watch the flickering candles and wait.

Omama returns an hour later.

"I have never seen so many people at synagogue," she says. "Some nice woman gave me her seat or else I would have been forced to stand on my terrible legs."

Mama and I exchange a small smile. We both know that Omama's legs suffer from nothing more than the ache of old age, although she has stiff and creaky hips.

We sit together at the table and Omama recites kiddush over cups of wine. It is supposed to be said by the man of the house, but Omama is now the senior in Papa's absence so she does it without being asked. She offers another prayer, dips chunks of challah into salt and passes it around.

We eat Mama's delicious food and try to ignore the bangs and screams coming from outside.

"Sing, Hanna," says Mama after we have finished the meal and ended with a prayer and another cup of wine. "Go on. 'Raisins and Almonds'. Sing it for Papa, no?"

I wish she hadn't mentioned his name. I'm going to

have a wobble in my voice when I sing now.

But Omama and Mama are looking at me, their faces shining with anticipation. So I take a breath, stand up and sing my favourite song in Yiddish, just to delight them even more.

When I've finished, Mama wipes away a tear.

"You are still Papa's little songbird," she says.

I smile because she's being a bit overemotional and I feel embarrassed.

"Oy," says Omama. "All this eating and praying has worn me out. I am off to my bed."

She hobbles out of the room, leaving Mama and me sitting in virtual darkness. We have extinguished the Sabbath candles with wine. It is part of our religious ritual.

It's nice, sitting together in the dark room. Or it would be if there were fewer strange noises coming from outside.

I can't think what I'm hearing. It's a muffled noise, like a radio in the distance with somebody turning up the volume dial a bit at a time. I can hear thin sounds of screaming.

There's a faint smell of smoke.

I am just thinking about going to bed and putting this confusing day behind me when there is another scream from right outside and a babble of concerned voices.

Mama leaps up and presses her face to the gap in the curtain.

"It is Rachel Solomon," she says. "I can't hear what she is saying. I'd better go down."

"No," I start to say, but Mama is already rushing outside. I look down and see her join the group of concerned people below, put her arm around Rachel's shoulder and say something to her. Whatever it is that Rachel says back to my mother causes her to drop to her knees like a stone and start to pray out loud in the street.

I run downstairs faster than I've ever run in my life.

"Mama!' I shout, pushing my way to her. "What has happened?"

My mother is crying so much that I can't understand what she is saying. With the help of another of our neighbours, Mr Bloom, I hoist Mama back into the apartment block and slowly up the stairs. I'm a bit worried about Mr Bloom because he's ninety, but he seems to have the stamina of a much younger man.

I wait until Mama has drunk some of the coffee I have made and then she holds out her hands to me and we sit close together on the sofa.

"Oh, Hanna," she says. "They have burned down the Great Choral Synagogue."

I start with horror. The Great Choral Synagogue on *Gogoļa iela* is one of the largest and oldest in all of Rīga.

"What?" I say. "No – it's a holy building. Nobody can burn it. Not even the Germans."

Tears pour down Mama's cheeks.

"Well, they have done it," she whispers. "And Hanna – three hundred Jews were locked inside."

The next day the rest of the shiny challah loaves sit untouched upon our table.

Chapter Four

Later that morning, Uldis picks me up and we head to the swimming baths in town.

I had dressed in a daze. We hadn't slept a wink and were still in shock from what had happened, but Omama told me to get cleaned up and put something nice on. Mama just said that there were other boys in the world and that I shouldn't get too hung up on the first one I've ever liked, but I ignored her.

So I am wearing a pair of khaki shorts and a white shirt knotted over my blue one-piece costume and it feels wrong even to be thinking about how I look.

In any case I feel a little shy having my legs out on display, but at least it is warm in the sunshine today.

I like the feeling of the sun on the crown of my head.

Seeing Uldis is like having balm applied to a sore spot, even though underneath the cut runs deep.

I have no idea whether mentioning what happened last night will risk ruining the mood of our date but I can't help but bring it up. I can talk to Uldis about anything.

"You will have heard the dreadful news about the Jews killed in the synagogue?" I say.

We are walking through the old town, my hand slipped through Uldis's arm. He is wearing brown trousers and a crisp white shirt and his hair is oiled back, ready for the swimming pool. In his hand is a small satchel containing his striped swimming trunks and a couple of towels.

"Oh yes," says Uldis. "It is truly tragic. I witnessed it all. Those poor people trapped inside."

I shudder.

"How come you saw it?" I say.

"I was passing by," says Uldis. His voice is low and sober.

We don't talk much after that. Even though we have been going out for a few months now, our relationship is still fragile and soft, like a newborn baby. It is enough to feel the sun on my skin and the muscle in Uldis's forearm under my hand. Before we started going out we were always messing about play-fighting and pushing and tickling one another and yet I never gave the physical contact a second thought.

Now I am shy of even having my hand on his warm arm.

Uldis greets people as we walk towards the pool. His family is well-connected in Rīga and his father knows all the business people in the city. Lots of men stop to shake his hand. Uldis is unfailingly polite and considerate, asking after elderly relatives and bending down to pat an assortment of small hairy dogs.

I feel proud to be with him.

He has his hand in the small of my back, guiding me through the door to the pool, letting me go first.

"You have lovely manners," I can't help saying. "That is why my papa liked you so much, I think."

Uldis blushes. I guess he's modest, too.

"Come on," he says. "Last one into the pool has to buy the ices!'

I'm so busy splashing my way up and down the centre of the pool and admiring Uldis as he jumps from the very highest diving board, his body all lean and hard like a whippet, that for a while I don't notice somebody staring at me from across the pool.

When I stop to catch my breath at the side and remove my goggles, I can see my best friend from ballet school, Velna, bobbing up and down in the deep end and looking over. She has her blonde plaits tied up on top of her head and is wearing a bright green swimsuit which sets off her flawless ivory skin.

"Velna," I call, waving my arms back and forth. "Come and swim with me!"

But the sound doesn't carry far enough, perhaps. I could have sworn she saw me, but maybe I am wrong. She has turned round and is deep in conversation with another group of girls I recognize from ballet school.

"Oh," I say. I chew on my lip, troubled. Uldis swims up underneath me and grabs me from behind, making me scream and kick out great streams of water.

"I think Velna is ignoring me," I tell him.

"Why would she do that?" says Uldis. "You are good friends."

"I thought we were," I say. For some reason I think of Poland when I say this.

"Don't worry about it," says Uldis. "She'll be fine when you next see her."

When he kisses me, all wet and fresh-faced and stares down at me with those hypnotic ice-blue eyes, I forget about Velna, the pool, Rīga, Latvia and everything else.

*

Mama keeps me away from dance school for nearly two weeks. She is afraid I will get caught up in all the shooting on the streets. But I feel caged in and desperate to stretch my limbs, so in the end I persuade her to let me go back.

Uldis offers to walk me as far as the river on my first day. My school is on the other side, which means I have to run across a busy traffic bridge; but it is not the cars that Mama is afraid of.

"You cannot go around the city alone," she says. "It is not safe now. I will walk over each day and fetch you from class. We can return home together."

I roll my eyes at her but I'm pleased that Uldis will be accompanying me on my first day back. Uldis has now joined the Latvian police and he looks very smart in his uniform. I enjoy being seen on his arm as I walk past the Freedom Monument and towards my school. I take sideways glances at his khaki uniform with the red and white patch armband, red stripes on the collar and the hat, with the Latvian insignia of three stars in the rays of a rising sun.

The only thing is that I keep remembering the young Jewish boys I saw being marched towards the prefecture by men in this very uniform. But I have never seen anything like that happen since and I know that Uldis has a heart of gold.

Just looking at that rising sun on his hat gives me hope.

"Why did you decide to join the police?" I ask Uldis. "I thought you were so keen to become a lawyer."

We are hurrying out of the old town and down *Kaļķu iela* towards the banks of the River Daugava. I get the feeling that Uldis is preoccupied with something this morning. He spends much time craning his neck and staring at people who pass us by.

I pinch my cheeks on the sly to get rid of my pale skin. We have had very little sleep over the past few nights because of the shootings and screaming. Mama has never again mentioned the synagogue but I read in *Tēvija* that nearly all the synagogues in Rīga have been burned now.

Ours is the only one which still stands. Omama says it is because the building is packed in close to other houses and offices in *Peitavas iela* right in the centre of the old town and that the Nazis wanted to use it as a store. Although she does not say what for, she tells me that Hitler believes that Jews are in league with the Communists and caused the defeat of Germany in World War I. As revenge he wants to get rid of all Jews.

I let out a gasp when she said that. I was doing a pirouette around the living-room floor at the time. There are millions of us Jews in the world! How can one man even begin to think of doing such a thing?

Then I thought of what happened in the Great Choral Synagogue and I stopped dancing out of respect for the victims.

Mama went pale and told me I shouldn't listen to Omama and that I should stop reading *Tēvija* because it is a Latvian publication set up to show sympathy with the Nazis. But I can't seem to stop reading it, especially when they print a new instruction in bold black letters, so I carry on sneaking it up to the apartment and reading it under the covers in bed. I want to know what is going on.

I wonder if Uldis reads *Tēvija*?

"I am proud to be Latvian, like my father and his father before him," says Uldis. He has taken his cap off and his fair hair catches the light of the sun. "I guess I am fighting to keep Latvia for the Latvians. I can always train to be a lawyer after the war."

He gives me his wide grin. I am reassured. With volunteers like Uldis in our police force, surely the Nazis will soon retreat from Rīga and let us get on with our lives?

We reach the bridge and see the large glass building on

the other side. My heart gives a little leap of nerves and joy. I've missed this place for the last two weeks.

I say goodbye to Uldis and stand on tiptoe to plant a quick kiss on his cheek.

"See you tomorrow," he says. "Have a great day."

"Of course I will," I say. "I love my dance classes."

Uldis kisses me back and walks away.

I stand by the morning rush-hour traffic and get the usual pang of sadness at our separation.

He is so handsome. I decide that I wouldn't much like it if he changed his mind about us being more than friends.

Then I run over the bridge towards my school.

There is an announcement before class begins.

The ballet mistress, in her dramatic long black skirt with the split up the side, claps her hands as we all lounge against the barre at the back of the hall. I'm standing on my own and wondering why Helena and Velna just came in and stood as far away as possible from me. We've been best friends since the very first day I entered this school a year ago. They are both blonde and tall with beautiful sharp bone structure in their faces but Helena has dark eyes and Velna's are brilliant blue. The three of us with our fair hair in buns are sometimes called "the triplets" and it's true, we do look similar. But Velna and Helena still have their fathers living safe at home and they have not had to move to an apartment or lose their families or their factories.

Already I feel that there is a gap widening between the two of them and me. I am starting to wonder if their fathers are reading *Tēvija* and believing some of the things that are written in there. But I don't think that my friends would be so narrow-minded as to believe them too.

"Girls, from today our academy is to be known under a new name," calls the ballet mistress. She stamps her stick on the floor to get absolute quiet. "We are no longer the School of the Opera and Ballet Theatre of LSSR. As from this moment we are the Rīga Opera Ballet School."

There's a murmur of surprise.

I go and stand next to Velna.

"What do you think?" I whisper. She shrugs.

"I guess it is because we are no longer under Soviet occupation," she says.

Velna sounds odd today. Distant, like she's not really talking to me.

"Hey, didn't you see me at the pool?" I mutter under my breath. "I was waving at you!"

Velna shrugs.

"So?" she says.

My heart jolts with shock. So she *did* see me. I'm about to ask her another question but the ballet mistress is glaring at me.

"There may be other changes," she says. She continues to stare in my direction when she says that. "But that is all for now. Assume your positions please, girls."

We run to the side of the room and begin to warm up, stretching our calves by placing our legs on top of the barre along the wall and bending towards them, straightening the ribbons on our shoes and curving our arms into graceful arches over our heads.

The rehearsal pianist in the corner starts to play a soft version of "The Dying Swan" from *Swan Lake*.

Then I hear a sharp laugh behind me. It is not a happy sound.

I turn around with one leg still swung up on top of the barre. Mama is always exclaiming at how flexible I am and telling me not to rip my leg from my hip socket.

I look straight into the face of Marija Otis. She has been the star of our class for the entire year. Her parents have dedicated their lives to getting her through this ballet school and towards a glittering future.

Marija could be a poster girl for all of Latvia with her honey-coloured hair, perfect high cheekbones and long neck.

"You know what she means by 'changes'," she whispers to me. "If not, you will soon enough."

The ballet mistress is passing us by. Marija dips her head down towards her feet in their tiny rose-pink pointe shoes and pretends to be rehearsing a piece from the ballet we're working on. When the teacher has moved on to the girl behind, she smoothes a stray wisp of blonde hair back into place on her perfect head and grabs my shoulder, forcing me to turn back towards her.

The hairs on my neck are standing up.

"Get off," I say. "What do you want?"

She gives her harsh laugh again.

"What would I want from you, you dirty Jew?" she says. "I want the same as everybody else in here. To get you out of our country."

I am so shocked that for a moment the room spins and I think, *I can't have heard that right.*

Dirty Jew.

Dirty Jew.

Dirty Jew.

"I was born in Rīga, same as you," I say. "I'm Latvian, just like you."

In answer, Marija spits a warm gob of phlegm right into my face.

The ballet mistress calls an extra break after that.

I expect her to chastise Marija or at least offer me some reassurance but all she does is shove a handkerchief at my face and click off in her black dance shoes towards the sanctity of the staff room.

Velna and Helena disappear out of the hall without looking back.

The other girls break up into groups and stand around whispering and staring over at me. Nobody comes to see if I am all right.

I'm in such a state of shock that at first I don't feel anything much at all. Then a creeping sick feeling starts to wrap its chill fingers around my heart.

These are my friends. Why do they no longer see me as Hanna?

Marija's words echo round my head all morning.

I want to run home to Mama and cry my heart out but there are other classes that I must endure.

I go to see if I can find Velna and Helena but they're nowhere to be seen.

Later on after the fuss has died down I am in a class with Helena and I go up to her and smile and try to be friendly, but she looks left and right with something a bit too close to fear in her eyes and she shuffles away from me like she might catch something and she says: "Sorry, but my parents have told me not to mix with Jews now.

I can't be seen talking to you any more."

"But I am only half Jewish!" I protest.

Helena is almost leaning backwards in her attempt not to be breathed on by the dirty Jew. Me.

"My mother says that if your mother is Jewish then you are wholly a Jew," she says. "Sorry."

Her apology is the least genuine that I've ever heard.

I somehow make it to the end of the day. Then I go into the ladies' lavatories and rip my hair out of its neat bun. I let it tumble all around my shoulders. I wipe off the pink lipstick and blue eyeshadow that the dancers here always wear. Then I pull off my rehearsal clothes – the tights and the white leotard, the little white wraparound skirt that I used to love wearing. I pull off my pointe shoes so hard that I snap a pink ribbon but I don't care.

I change into my sweater and boring knee-length skirt, put on my flat brown brogues and leave my hair wild and loose.

I look at myself for a good long while in the mirrors. I do not look dirty. I do not even look much like a Jew.

"You are Hanna Michelson," I say. "That is who you are."

My voice comes out just like Papa's. It is strong and proud, but underneath I don't feel as if I'll ever smile again.

Underneath I am crumbling faster than one of Mama's vanilla cookies.

Then I push open the heavy doors of the ballet school and let them bang behind me.

It's almost the summer holidays anyway.

But I know I'll never go back.

Chapter Five

I GET HOME VERY EARLY. I have a headache and feel about twenty years older than when I left home that morning.

Mama is bent over her sewing machine when I return to the apartment.

She is working with silver bugle beads. Mama often sews these tiny tubes around the neckline or hem of a wedding dress. She has to use good light and her spectacles to ensure that they are sewn on with precision.

I notice that her right hand is not as steady as usual.

She jumps when I come into the room.

"Hanna!" she says. "I am supposed to come and collect you! Why are you home?"

Omama is sitting in her chair in the corner of the room, humming to herself and reading a copy of *Tēvija* even though Mama has tried to ban it from the apartment. "It tells us what is going on," protests Omama whenever Mama snatches the paper away from her. "It tells us what might be in store for us next."

"That is why I don't want to read it," says Mama.

All the way home from dance school I made myself promise not to upset Mama.

But when I see her dark head lowered over the sewing machine from our old house, something twangs with pain in my memory. I see Papa standing smiling in the doorway with his shirtsleeves rolled up and his strong brown arms stretched out towards me.

I collapse into sobs at the dining-room table and drop my head onto my arms.

Mama puts her white fabric down in alarm.

"Hanna, what is it?" she says. Omama has struggled over and is attempting to do one of her painful cheek-pinches, even though my cheeks are already a horrid red from crying.

I tell them what happened at school.

Omama shakes her head in disgust.

"*Ach, Gott,*" she says. "These girls don't possess a brain cell between them. Pay no attention, Hanna. Go back with your head held high."

Mama says nothing. Her eyes have dark patches

underneath them from not sleeping. I can't help noticing that in the pile of work she keeps in the corner, there is hardly anything left to do.

"People don't want a Jew touching their clothing," she says, following my gaze. "Only Jewish customers will come to me now and many of them are already talented with a needle."

I swallow hard. If Mama has no work, then what will we do for food?

Omama reads my mind.

"Don't fret, little one," she says. "I have some jewels hidden away. If I need to sell them, I will."

"And I have some as well," says Mama. "I managed to smuggle them from the villa. So we will eat. Of course we will eat! What would we be without our food, huh?"

I smile, just a little. But Velna's mocking expression and the feeling of Marija's warm gob of phlegm on my cool cheeks replay in my mind over and over. I feel dirty – tainted – by her having done that to me.

"You will get back to your dance school," says Mama. "This madness will not last long. The war won't go on for much longer. Already we have had that year of Soviet occupation and now this. So we will soon be back to our villa and our normal life, yes?"

I nod. She hasn't mentioned Papa.

His absence looms even larger.

I feel lonely, for the first time in my life. All the normal things – Papa, the villa, dance school, even food – are being stripped away one by one.

Later I wipe my tears away and help Mama by winding cotton reels and sorting needles. Omama brings in some black bread and cheese and we eat in companionable silence.

Except that outside, it is never silent now.

Uldis treats me to an afternoon film at the cinema.

It is mid July and Rīga is at its most beautiful, with colourful flowers along the roadsides and in the park and a dry, hot sun which brings out groups of young people all over town.

"To cheer you up after what happened at dance class," he says as he pays for the tickets.

I glow with an unexpected happiness. I have his sweater around my shoulders and despite the ballet class I feel lucky. I have Uldis and I have Mama and Omama and I reckon that even though I miss Papa so much that it makes me feel sick, I am still cherished and loved by those three important people.

So I let him buy me a box of chocolates at the cinema and we sit in the very back row with his arm draped around me. I enjoy sniffing the clean smell of the nape of his neck and the film is a silly comedy so we both laugh and I block out the thoughts of my Jewish blood and the mocking look on the face of Marija Otis and for two hours I just enjoy being with my favourite person in the world.

Uldis.

My happy mood is not allowed to last for long.

I go home for the evening, as Mama has told me that we will try to celebrate the Sabbath as usual.

Mama has queued for hours in disguise again.

She comes home with only some grey fish, which smells as if it has been in the shop for too long, and a lump of black bread which is so stale that I can't get the knife through it. There are some small hard potatoes which don't boil soft, so the potato salad becomes bullet salad even when disguised with Mama's home-made dressing of lemon and vinegar.

There is no meat to make cholent for Saturday lunch tomorrow and there is no white flour to make the shiny plaited challah loaves either. Mama is distraught about this, but Omama tells her it doesn't matter. That surprises me – Omama is far more religious than Mama.

"It matters only that we are all together," she says. "We have enough food to stay alive. For that we should be grateful."

"Yes, yes," mutters Mama. She is so proud of her cooking and her neat kitchen. I can see that it pains her to serve up hard potatoes and less-than-fresh fish.

I lay the Sabbath table. No fresh flowers this time. But I light the candles and we say the blessing and pour a little wine.

Omama does not go to synagogue. Although her *Peitav Shul* is the only one still standing, rumour has it that the Nazis have ripped out the holy parchment scrolls clad in velvet and silk and burned them, along with the holy books and prayer shawls and all the ornate brocade curtains and hangings inside.

Omama can't bear to talk about it.

So she says her prayers at the table and we sit together and eat the small meal that Mama has managed to pull together. Omama has problems managing potatoes or bread with her false teeth but Mama produces some leftover sponge cake and she chomps away on that instead.

Outside the sounds of shooting and screaming punctuate the heat of the night, even though Mama has shut the window and drawn the thick drapes. She blocks out the sight of our beloved St Peter's burned to a grey windowless stump. I can barely remember what it looked like before.

When we have used the last of the wine to put out the candles and Mama has washed the plates, we sit down in our living room. Mama resumes some needlework, I put on my ballet shoes and practise my grand plié in the corner. I point my legs out in opposite directions and bend my knees with care, keeping my back straight and the movement as fluid as I can. Then I perform an élevé – a gentle lift right up onto the balls of my feet. Because the flat is carpeted and we have neighbours below, I'm not allowed to do any jetés but I can imagine them in my head.

Mama smiles at me over the top of her spectacles.

"That's the spirit," she says. "You must always carry on your dancing, Hanna. You will go back to school in September."

I stand on one leg and tip the other one right up towards my head.

"Oy, oy," says Omama, wincing. I snatch a look at her bony brown legs. The kneecaps are pointing in different directions. I can't imagine Omama dancing, or even being young. But I guess she must have been, once. There's a grainy photo by her bed of a woman with soft brown curls which escape from an ornate bun. She has large brown eyes and a tiny waist shown off in a nipped-in long dress and she stands tall and proud and wide-hipped, not bent over and thin. When Mama told me who it was, I found it difficult to believe her.

I'm not going to get old like that. I will look just the same as I do now, except for a few grey hairs in my long fair plait. I will still be dancing, just like I promised Papa. I will look after Mama when she gets old, because I promised Papa that, too.

But I will never let old age happen to me in that way.

When I have set my mind to something I can be very stubborn.

I have a phrase I use that Papa always used to tease me for: I have decided!

That evening I wait until Mama and Omama have gone to bed.

Then I make myself a hot cup of coffee and pull out Omama's hidden copy of *Tēvija.*

Just looking at the thick bold black font that they use for their headlines makes me feel sick in the pit of my stomach, but I can't seem to stop. I am becoming obsessed with this paper. I tell myself that I need to know what is going on because I promised Papa that I would look after Mama. It makes me feel kind of weary and adult.

I switch on my bedside lamp and hug my knees up towards my chest. I open the copy of *Tēvija* and sip the black coffee.

The very first line makes me catch my breath.

In thick black text that seems to leap out and hurt my eyes, it says this:

The Jewish sins are gross: they wanted to destroy our nation and, therefore, must perish as a culture.

I close the paper with a shaking hand and get out of bed. I kneel by the bed in the dark and I close my eyes and pray to God.

I ask Him to tell us what our sins are and that He might forgive them so that we don't have to suffer.

Perish as a culture.

I dissect the words and make them separate again. On their own they mean nothing. I put them together in the wrong order. They still mean nothing.

Culture. As. Perish. A.

A. Culture. Perish. As.

Then I put them back together.

Perish as a culture.

I lie awake for hours with my heart thudding.

The noise of breaking glass and anguished screams goes on for the rest of the night.

Chapter Six

THERE ARE NEW RULES FOR the Jews of Rīga and things are getting worse.

There are not many shops where Jews are allowed to buy food now and there are members of Hitler's *Schutzstaffel* soldiers from the Nazi party keeping armed guard on the streets.

Sometimes they open fire on a Jewish man or woman without warning. Mama has seen people lying dead or injured at the side of the road and she's frightened to let me go outside at all now.

I try not to look at the bodies, because they make me feel sick with fear, but it's difficult. There are so many.

I feel like I'm going mad stuck inside this apartment with very little fresh air.

I haven't been anywhere. I so miss my Saturday swimming sessions with Uldis but it's too risky to leave the apartment.

I'm still reeling from the sentence I read in the paper just over two weeks ago. Since then I have met up only once with Uldis in town after Mama ran into him and he said he was missing me and that he would take me out for a walk in the fresh air.

Mama had taken some convincing, but in the end she agreed after Omama pointed out that I was looking pale. So I walked with my beloved Uldis through the cobbled streets of Vecrīga and I felt safe with him being in his policeman's uniform.

I took great deep breaths of the balmy summer air and got so dizzy that I had to stop and steady myself on an old building for a second. I had missed being outside, but not as much as I'd missed Uldis.

"It's good to see you," I said. The time we had for the walk seemed very short and precious and I wanted to tell him my feelings straight away.

"Sorry," said Uldis. "I have been busy with my police work. It's really good to see you too, Hanna."

Uldis looked around at other people a lot while we were walking. At one point he stared hard at an armoured vehicle where four of those SS men were sitting smoking and watching the people walk by. One of the men stared back at him and made a gesture I couldn't understand.

"What was that about?" I said. "Are you working for the SS now?"

Uldis laughed.

"Of course not," he said. "I am not a German. I will look after you, Hanna. That is all that matters."

I went quiet for a moment. I had put on my prettiest dress for the trip out and I was hurting that Uldis hadn't noticed the red flowers on the white fabric or the neat belt that Mama had made me to cinch my waist in. For a moment I had a horrid feeling of doubt about our relationship and whether he liked me as much as I liked him.

But by the time Uldis saw me back to the apartment door we were chatting away again, just like we always did. We walked close, pressed up against one another, and the feeling of his hard thigh in the rough uniform was exciting against my own soft leg.

"When will I see you again?" I called after him.

Uldis turned round and gave me his lopsided, bright grin.

"Soon," he called back. "Take care, Hanna. My regards to your mama and omama."

*

Mama comes back from one of her dangerous trips into town to queue for food and she is clutching a rotten lemon and a piece of paper.

"These are pinned up all around town," she says. "Look."

With a trembling hand she puts the crumpled piece of paper, still with a pin through its heart, on the table in front of us.

We peer at it in silence.

Regulation One:
Jews are prohibited from visiting public places: swimming pools, parks and all city facilities.
Jews are prohibited from using cinemas, theatres, libraries or museums.
Jews are prohibited from owning trucks, cars or radios.
Women Jews are prohibited from wearing hats or using umbrellas.
Jews are ordered only to use Jewish doctors or dentists.
Jews are entitled to only half the food rations of non-Jews.

Regulation Two:

All Jews must wear on the left breast a six-pointed yellow star which must measure ten centimetres wide. Violation of this regulation is punishable by death.

We stare at one another.

The last line seems so unreal that at first I ignore it.

Punishable by death.

No. It can't be true.

I push it from my mind and glance instead at the pile of library books I have taken out over the last two weeks. Will I get fined if I am not allowed to enter the library to take them back?

Then I think about those Saturday swims I so enjoy with Uldis. I am banned from using the baths because I am a Jew. He will still be able to go there, but without me. What if he meets another girl there and forgets about me?

I feel sick thinking this, so I get up and move about to break my train of thought.

I look at Mama and wonder how she will be able to walk the streets of Rīga without her hat or umbrella. It is the beginning of the humid, rainy season in Rīga and the water can come down in sheets at times.

I glance at Omama. She is clutching the radio she likes

to listen to at night. I think she tries to tune in to folk music to remind her of her youth in Talsi, a tiny village several miles outside Rīga.

Mama breaks the frozen moment. She goes over to her sewing box and gets out a roll of yellow fabric and her pair of large scissors. She gestures to me to find black cotton from her tin of cotton reels and we sit down at the table.

Nobody speaks.

I watch Mama snip the fabric into the shape of a star and hold it against her tape measure.

When she has finished, three perfect yellow Star of David badges sit on the table in front of us.

Omama picks one up.

"We should be proud to wear this," she says. "It is the star of our faith. They can't break us down in this way."

Mama shakes her head and sighs.

"They are trying to mark us out as different," she says. "And it is working. How will I queue now for food if they see my star?"

"You will have to find shops without queues," I say. We all know that this is impossible.

Mama gets me to find my school jacket. She sews the star onto the left breast and stands back to admire her handiwork.

"You will always have to wear this jacket outside now,"

she says. "Even on a hot day such as this."

Punishable by death. The unspoken words bounce between us.

I pull a face. I picture myself walking with Uldis and having to ruin my pretty summer dress by wearing this jacket over the top.

Then I think: *But where would we go on our date? I can no longer enter a cinema or theatre or even walk with him in the park by the canal.*

I feel short of breath. The walls of our apartment seem to be closing in.

Mama sees just in time and gets me to put my head between my knees.

She strokes my hot hair off my sweaty forehead and brings me a drink of water.

When I have stopped feeling dizzy she sews Omama's star onto a black coat with red stitching around the hem. Then she sews her own star onto the navy coat she wears for best.

Omama goes to bed clutching her radio in defiance. I know full well that she's going to listen to it all night and turn the volume up extra-loud.

"You must get rid of that," Mama tells her. "What if one of our neighbours hears it and reports us to the authorities?"

Not all of the residents in our block are Jewish. I have noticed that some people have stopped talking to us if they pass us on the stairs. They rush off like frightened rabbits pursued by a ruthless fox. I want to tell them that it's the other way around – that we are the frightened ones, pursued by a hostile band of Nazis.

Omama flaps her arms as if to get Mama to go away. She is not frightened. At least, not in the way that Mama and I are. Omama told me last week that she has lived through another World War, eviction from several of her homes and several pogroms where Jews were shot on the streets. She has even survived a five-year expulsion to Russia.

Omama thinks that she is indestructible.

I only hope she's right.

It seems I no longer have a best friend. Velna has ignored me ever since that day at ballet school and even when I saw her on the street when I came out of the cinema with Uldis, she turned her blonde head away and crossed over to the other side.

It hurts like hell. We used to tell each other everything and now I have nobody to confide my feelings about Uldis to. Mama seems to disapprove of Uldis more than ever and is starting not to be able to hide it but I daren't ask her why. I suppose it is just because the difference between Jews and non-Jews is getting greater by the day. When she gets that tight-lipped look it is very difficult to say anything to her at all. Omama likes Uldis and will talk to me about him but she sees him as just a young boy.

The apartment starts to close in on me even more.

Our villa was large and spacious, but this tiny flat is lacking in air and the small amount that is left seems to be soaked into the fabric of the chairs, curtains and carpets.

Because we no longer have quite enough to fill our stomachs I spend a lot of time with a strange aching sick feeling in my guts which doesn't help. I can't seem to sleep properly without a full stomach.

I pace up and down, peering out of the window until Mama puts down her work, takes off her spectacles and gives me an appraising look.

Omama retreats into her bedroom, still clutching the illegal radio.

"All right, you win," Mama says. "You can take these alterations back to Mrs Kronis. Just make sure your star is visible at all times and stay away from the soldiers. Don't stop to talk to anyone. Come straight back. Okay?"

"Yes, yes," I say. I've already got my jacket on and am standing by the door with my arms full of dresses and skirts.

"If you see a shop with no queue, try to get us some bread," says Mama. "I realize that this is about as likely as the war finishing this afternoon, but still, you could try."

I'm halfway down the stairs.

I walk through the burned-out streets of the city I love.

There is a feeling of mistrust and worry in the air. People huddle along with their heads kept low. They no longer stop to admire the art nouveau buildings with their carved heads and cats or browse through the street markets.

On every street corner there is a patrol, some with cars where Hitler's SS soldiers sit and watch the population go by. Omama refers to them as "those Nazi bastards", and tends to spit whenever she mentions them. Latvian policemen stride up and down the pavements with their guns hoisted high and no time for the neighbours they used to socialize with.

I try to imagine Uldis, grim and unsmiling, with a gun, and it doesn't seem possible.

My heart gives a little jump when I think I see him, except it's another Latvian policeman with similarly chiselled cheekbones and fair hair.

I am heading to the home of Maya Kronis. She is a friend of Mama's who lives on the other side of the old town. Her sight is failing and she cannot see to thread a needle, so Mama does all her mending at a reduced rate.

I hurry past the *Doma laukums*, our grand cathedral. So far it has escaped the bombing and fire. I pass the *Trīs brāļi,* three houses which stand together but are all from different centuries. I knock on Mrs Kronis's door on *Klostera iela.* Mrs Kronis still lives in her own house. I feel envious of her three floors and pretty backyard.

"Hanna," she says, opening her front door only wide enough to put her nose through it. "How kind of you to come across town with my clothes. Please send my best wishes to your mother. You will understand if I don't ask you in today?"

"Oh," I say. "Yes."

I'm a little disappointed and thirsty, having crossed town in the sticky heat of July in a black jacket.

Mrs Kronis opens the door just wide enough to grab her clothes and then shuts it with an apologetic shrug.

I walk back through town at a snail's pace. Because I

am out of breath, hot and tired, I notice more on the way back than I did on the way there.

Several people stare at me in an odd way. Others cross to the other side of the road, pulling their clothes around themselves as if I am a virus that might penetrate through to their skin.

Some of these people are classmates from my ballet school or friends of Mama's from way back when we lived in the villa.

I see Velna's mother hurrying along across the street with a shopping basket and so I call out "Hello!" and give her a wave, as she has always been very kind to me whenever I visited Velna after school for tea.

Velna's mother gives a little jump and hugs her basket to her chest as if I'm about to run over and grab it from her. She stops for a moment and half opens her mouth. Then she lowers her head and rushes on without looking back.

My heart aches with shock and sadness.

I look down at the star on my left breast. It is very yellow against the black of my jacket. I feel as if I might be glowing. Squinting down at it gives me an ice-cream headache and a pain in the back of my neck so I stop.

I feel different. I feel as if Rīga is no longer my place of birth.

It is my city, but it is as if I've come down from another planet. Familiar buildings look strange. My feet echo on the pavement with a hollow snapping sound that I have never noticed before.

There are other Jews wearing stars.

I try to catch their eye and smile as I pass them but very few people react and, if they do, it's with a guilty half-smile as if they've been caught doing something they shouldn't have.

Omama told me to wear the star with pride because it is a symbol of our faith, but I don't feel proud.

I just feel embarrassed.

When I get home to the apartment I rip the jacket off and burst into tears.

"I don't want to be Jewish," I say, lying face down on my bed with Mama perching on the edge. "I want to be like Papa. I am going to be Latvian and not Jewish from now on. I will not wear the star. I look Latvian. I could get away with it."

Mama looks as if she is considering something. Then she shakes herself, as if trying to get out of a trance, and pulls me into a sitting position and holds my hands. I notice the pale skin around her knuckles and the way that her gold wedding band is swivelling around her finger. It is getting loose.

"Oh, Hanna," she says. "I am afraid that as far as Jewish law goes, you are considered to be Jewish if your mother is. You must never go out without your star now."

"Is that what Hitler thinks too?" I say. "Because I have Papa's blood in me too, remember?"

We are both silent for a moment. I can see Mama wrestling with painful images of Papa, just like I am. I can see him grinning at me over breakfast and ruffling my hair. Sometimes at night I almost feel him sitting by my bed, watching me sleep.

"I'm sorry," says Mama. "I'm sorry you have to be Jewish at this terrible time. There is nothing I can do to alter that fact. It is who you are."

She takes me into the kitchen to make me a warm drink.

"Oh," she says, stirring a cup of hot chocolate. "The money from Mrs Kronis – could you put it in my tin?"

I start in horror. With the strangeness of everything in town I quite forgot to ask Mrs Kronis for the mending money.

Mama sees my face and sighs.

"Never mind," she says. "These are strange times. Easy to forget what normal is, yes?"

I can't help noticing when she opens the cupboard to put the tin of hot chocolate away that there are lots of gaps where there used to be packets and boxes of food.

"Are we going to run out of food, Mama?" I say.

My question coincides with the arrival of Omama fresh from her afternoon nap.

"Run out of food?" she says, slapping my arm. "Run out of food? Not while I've got breath in my old body, girl!"

She disappears off back into her bedroom and then emerges with a slim box of biscuits which she proceeds to arrange in patterns on a plate with great deliberation and much muttering.

"I have friends in high places," is all she'll say when we quiz her about where the biscuits have come from.

We laugh. Omama is full of surprises.

But that night I worry about the empty cupboards.

Then I replay Velna's expression for the hundredth time.

It's like everything is pushing me in a direction I really don't want to go.

When I go to bed I try to find a comfortable position but I can't.

I feel as if I am still wearing the Jewish star.

Chapter Seven

THERE ARE NEW OFFICIALS ON the street.

They wear white armbands with a blue Star of David on them. Some of them have long beards and skullcaps on.

Mama says that they are a special Jewish council set up to help the Nazis keep control over the rest of us. She says that they are on our side and that if we have any problems or questions our council members will be able to help us.

Omama snorts when Mama says this.

"I have been around too long," is all that she will say.

By August there is a new list of regulations pinned up in the street and emblazoned in big black letters all over the front page of *Tēvija.*

Regulations for Jews
All Jews must wear a second yellow star in the middle of their backs.
No Jew is permitted to walk on the sidewalks.

I look outside. I don't have to wait long. A steady stream of Jews is picking its way through the gutters outside. Horses and army vehicles roar past them, splattering them with the rain, ash and mud which now lie heavy over our streets.

Some of the Jews look dejected. Others have their heads held high. I can see that they are defiant and that they are trying to wear the star with what is left of their pride. Then I see them being whipped by Nazi soldiers for impertinence. I let out a cry and put my hands over my mouth. The Jews stumble to the ground and fall to their knees in the mud and rain. Some of them are whipped again and again and then kicked. They lie motionless in the gutter. The SS utter their loud barking laughs and move on. The lucky ones get up again and continue to walk.

Now their heads are bent low and they are limping.

Tears of anger rise up in my eyes. I notice that the new members of the Jewish Council are still allowed to walk on the pavements and use the buses and cabs.

"That's not fair," I say, out loud.

"Come away," says Mama, shooing me back into the room and pulling the curtains tight so that there is no gap. "Help me with the sewing, please."

She has the roll of yellow fabric out again. In silence I help her cut thread and measure the width of the stars to a perfect ten centimetres. Then she sews the three new stars onto the backs of our jackets.

"Well," says Omama, holding her coat up to admire Mama's handiwork. "Whatever next? They will have us dressing in giant star costumes soon."

We giggle, despite the solemnity of the moment.

Omama has a way with words.

Uldis comes to visit me.

Because of the way that the Nazis are beating and whipping us Jews on the streets I am imprisoned inside the apartment again at the moment. Uldis has been busy with his police work but he comes by on the way home sometimes and Mama begrudgingly cuts him the smallest piece of bread or sponge cake if she has managed to somehow make one out of almost no ingredients.

"Could you bring us food?" I ask him. It's all I can think about at the moment. "You must still be able to buy normal provisions."

Uldis sighs.

"Even for non-Jews there is not so much food about," he says. "The war is having an effect everywhere. But I will see if we have anything that we can spare."

"Oh," I say, disappointed. Sure, it's good to see him looking so well and handsome but I was hoping he might at least have brought us a cake. Mama's neck is getting scrawnier by the day and Omama spends more time sitting in a chair than she used to.

"It's all right," says Mama in a low voice. "We don't need your charity, Uldis. Hanna enjoys your visits so that will have to do for now."

Her face doesn't invite argument, so I pass Uldis a scrap of black bread and press my shoulder up against his.

A notice comes through our door.

It proclaims that all Jews must register with their local police stations.

"For what?" I say.

Mama passes me the piece of paper. Her hand has developed a tremor over the last week and I notice that she can never sit still for more than a minute at a time.

The paper says that all able-bodied Jews between fourteen and sixty-five must go out to work and will be assigned to jobs which they are not allowed to turn down.

"That is me, then," I say. "What will I *do*? All I can *do* is dance."

I have been trying to do my ballet exercises late at night when nobody is watching. I force my legs to go into first position and then work my way through to fifth before running through a series of arm exercises. There is precious little room for pirouetting in my tiny bedroom but I risk it anyway.

Mama sits down and puts her head in her hands for a moment.

"I don't know, Hanna," she says. "There will not be much choice in the matter."

"Who will look after Omama?" I say.

"Omama will," says Omama. "I am quite capable of amusing myself until your return. I can catch up with my ancient friends in this very building. I have my papers and radio and enough biscuits to see me by until these Nazi bastards have gone."

Mama rolls her eyes.

"Language, please," she says. "And that radio is supposed to be confiscated," she says. "Mama, you are awful."

But she is smiling.

*

We have to go to our local police station to register for work.

For the first time we are out on the streets with many of our Jewish neighbours. We haven't seen most of them for months. Mama uses the opportunity to speak to as many of her old friends as possible. I cling onto Omama's arm in the long queue outside the police station. She is too old to register for work and only came with us out of sheer nosiness. I'm clinging for safety but I'm also trying to hold her up without letting her know that this is what I'm doing.

Omama's legs are as thin as my arms now. We haven't had a lot of food over the last few weeks so now they look even more brittle, like small shiny brown twigs. Like the other Jewish women out here on the streets she is huddled inside a black headscarf as hats are no longer allowed and she is wearing her jacket with the two stars, just like everybody else. The queue outside the police station weaves its way like a dark wriggling snake covered in yellow splodges. The rain falls onto us and steam rises from the gutter. I have no hat or umbrella so my fair plait is becoming dark from the rain and my face shines with rainwater.

Mama is deep in conversation with an old friend, Mrs Brauner. From the way they are gesticulating and huddling together I can tell that the information Mama is receiving is causing her some distress.

Before I have a chance to creep nearer and eavesdrop the queue jolts forward and we find ourselves propelled through the door by the crowd. Omama pushes her way back outside.

Inside a small room there are men with white and blue armbands sitting behind a desk. I recognize some of them from our Jewish community.

We take our turn at the desk.

A man shoves two blue cards at us and gives us a pencil.

We have to fill in our place of residence and which apartment we live in. Then we have to put down our "present employment". I glance up at Mama in panic.

"Put down that you are a seamstress," she hisses. "I will teach you. Write it down. Quick."

I pencil the words with a trembling hand.

We are told that soon we will be placed in employment and that there is no choice in the matter. Then we are gestured to leave the room.

It isn't until we are outside rushing through the rain that something strikes me.

"Mama," I say, "why did we answer all the questions in pencil? Why not pen?"

We are approaching our apartment on *Skārņu iela.* I am holding onto Omama's arm to stop her stumbling.

"I don't know, Hanna," says Mama. "Maybe they do not want to keep a permanent record."

We both fall silent, considering what her words could imply.

She stops in the gutter to stare up at the window where we have spent so much time watching the destruction of our beautiful city. I see the rain pour down her cheeks and from the flushed colour of her skin and redness around her eyes I realize that the rainwater is mixing with tears.

Papa's face floats between us for a moment, as it often does. The three of us are sitting around the table in our elegant villa. The double doors are thrown open and the garden is full of birdsong and the smell of cherry blossom.

I reach for Mama's hand. I remember the promise I made to Papa.

"Don't worry," I say. "We will stick together. So we will be all right. And Papa will come home again when the war is over."

Mama cannot speak, but she grips my hand tighter.

"So much change ahead," is all she says, but it's enough to make the air take on a colder feel around our heads.

We duck inside our apartment block to get away from the rain.

*

Mama spends the next two weeks trying to teach me to sew.

I've already watched her for years as she makes and alters dresses, trousers and skirts, but watching it and doing it are two very different things. Although I've helped cut out patterns and sort fabrics, I realize that doing the sewing requires good co-ordination between my arms and my feet on the pedal.

"It's not fair," I say, as Mama tells me off for the hundredth time for messing up my stitches. Thread is flying all over the place and I've nearly stitched through my hand by putting it too close to the needle. "Why can I get my arms and legs to match in ballet but not here?"

Omama is trying to stifle a laugh.

"You are the worst seamstress I have ever seen," she crows. "It is a good job you are going to become a ballerina."

"Here," says Mama in a voice which she is trying very hard to keep patient. "Put it here. Like this. See? Then move it like this..." and she glides the fabric smoothly under the dipping needle. Her move is precise and confident. When I do it, the fabric catches and jerks and snarls up into lumps.

"It is like your dancing," she says. "At first it is difficult. But with practice it becomes easy, no?"

I shrug. My eyes ache from staring at the tiny stitches and my back hurts from hunching over the sewing table with my foot pumping up and down.

Deep down I miss dancing so much that I can hardly bear to think about it. My dreams seem to have been suspended somewhere just out of my reach and I can't touch them any longer. Sometimes at night I risk doing a few gentle jetés on the carpeted floor of my bedroom but my legs are losing muscle tone and I'm worried I will never be able to catch up again.

"Must I carry on learning this sewing?" I say. "Can't I get some other job?"

Omama's smile fades. She gets up and draws the curtains.

"You want to clean toilets for some Nazi soldier?" she says. "Because there will be plenty of those jobs for pretty young girls like you."

I shudder.

Then I bend over the fabric with an exaggerated sigh.

"Right," I say. "Let's start again."

August comes and with it the first truly hot days of summer.

We have still not been called to begin work. So we are sweltering up in the apartment and living on bread and cheese and black coffee or anything that Mama can get during her weekly trawl around the shops. Most of the shops have signs in the window proclaiming that no Jews are allowed to shop in there. There is very little food in the few shops allocated for us and what is there is often covered in a light dusting of green and yellow mould.

Uldis drops in when he can but he is busy. He tells me that the police have increased his hours of work. The streets are so dangerous that I can no longer choose to go and find him and must rely upon his visits. I am worried that because of this, we will grow apart. When he does visit he is as kind and polite as ever but the feeling in the air between us has changed. I'm guessing that it's partly because having a girlfriend who can't leave her apartment is restrictive for him, but there's something else. It makes me feel uncomfortable and when he leaves, I am both sorry and relieved in equal measures.

The relieved bit makes me feel sad.

I lie in bed and pray to God that we can carry on our romance as before.

Another thing is worrying me. A change has come over my mother and grandmother.

They will not let me near *Tēvija* any longer. Omama

takes it off into her bedroom to read. After reading the 23rd August edition she came out looking pale and frightened. She and Mama have taken to muttering in the corner of the lounge after I go to bed, only they often forget to shut the door so I can hear them if I strain my ears.

I am not stupid. I watch from our window as the lines of Jewish people pull carts and wheelbarrows along in the gutter and I can see that they have mattresses and suitcases crammed into these barrows. Where they are going, I do not know.

Mama knows, I think.

I ask her if we will soon have to put all our possessions in a cart and leave our home.

But she will not answer my questions. She paces up and down the apartment, glancing outside every now and then and grabbing onto her own elbows and scowling. It is like she is having an inner argument with herself. I wish I knew what she was thinking.

Sometimes I hate being treated like a child.

At the beginning of September I go on one of my rare walks outside. We have a curfew now which means we cannot be outside past six o'clock in the evening, but it is only four and it is a beautiful day and I have been allowed to go out so long as I wear my jacket.

I end up near the *Opera* in the beautiful park. Jews are not supposed to go into parks any longer but it draws me like a magnet. There are no soldiers around so I creep in and sit on a bench for half an hour and try to ignore the sounds of army vehicles rumbling down the *Brīvības bulvāris*.

I am sweating in my black jacket. It is boiling hot. I glance left and right and then with pleasure at the gleaming white building of the *Opera* where one day I will dance onstage and bow down for all the applause.

Or at least, I used to hope that I would. Now it feels less certain. Jews are not allowed to do anything which they once used to enjoy.

I can't bear the thought of not dancing. I don't really know what else to do with my life. It is what I am good at and what I love to do.

I take off my jacket with the yellow stars and lay it on the bench next to me. As soon as I slip it off I feel better. I am not Hanna the Jew with the yellow stars, I am just Hanna. I sit in my summer dress with the pink and white checked pattern and I hold my face up to the sun and drift off somewhere far away from my troubled city.

It is so hot that I go to sleep for a moment or two.

Then a sharp click makes me jolt back to the present.

The sun is blocked out. For a moment my dazed eyes can't work out what has happened. Then I see a uniform in front of me. My eyes adjust. I raise them up and see a cap with a pair of eagle's wings in gold. Then I frown. Under the eagle's wings is what looks like a badge in the shape of a skull.

It is a member of the SS.

I struggle into an upright position.

The soldier has a lazy grin on his face.

"Good afternoon," he says in a polite voice that reminds me a little of Uldis. "What a beautiful day to be sitting in the park."

I nod. Then I see another group of soldiers standing behind him. They are all grinning with that same, lazy interest.

I figure that if they're smiling, they can't be out to cause any trouble.

"I am a dance student," I say. "I am going to dance there one day."

I point at the *Opera* behind him.

The soldier doesn't even follow my finger. He is still leering at my face.

"You speak very good German, *Fräulein,"* he says. "And yet I see your coat has the yellow stars."

I flush and glance down at my jacket next to me.

"I was too hot," I say. "I have been wearing it all day. I am going to put it on again in a moment. I just wanted to feel the sun on my arms."

The soldier pulls out the long brown gun from his holster with a swift movement. For one crazy moment I think: *This is it. He is going to shoot me.*

He uses the muzzle of his gun to hook up my jacket. It hangs shapeless and black. He dangles it in front of my nose and gestures at me to take it.

"You do not make the rules, Jew," he says. The polite smile has never left his face. "Soon you will realize that."

My hands have started to tremble but I slide my arms into the jacket and pull it close about me. The cloth is cold and heavy on my sweating arms.

"Good afternoon," says the soldier with a sharp little bow. Then he joins the others and they walk off. The sound of their harsh laughter floats back to me on the summer breeze.

I cannot move.

I stay on the bench in my hot coat. I can feel the stars glowing yellow. They seem to pulsate in time to the beating of my heart.

After what seems an eternity, I leave the park and run home along the gutters.

Mama will be worried. I have been out far too long.

Chapter Eight

WHEN I GET HOME I lie on the bed and give way to my tears.

Mama sits next to me like she did when I was little. She is hunched over and fiddling with her wedding ring again.

"You were out so long," she says. "I was worried. Even Omama was worried. You must not stay out so long now. Things are not safe."

I pass my hand over my hot face to mop up the tears. I want to tell Mama about what just happened but something tells me that this will only make her more afraid.

"Mama," I say, "I don't want Jewish blood in me any longer. I want to take it out of my veins! I only want Papa's blood in me! How do I get the Jewish blood out?"

Mama's own eyes fill with tears. It is too late. I realize now what my words have just done to her.

"I am sorry, Hanna," she says in a voice kept firm with a lot of effort. "We have already had this conversation. You are my daughter and we can't change that fact. And you should be proud to be Jewish."

I dissolve into fresh tears.

"Proud?" I say. "When I am made to walk in the gutter and wear this STAR" – and here I rip off my jacket and hurl it across the room – "and I have to leave dance school and I never even see Uldis any more?"

I wish I hadn't said that last bit. It's a private pain that's been worrying me for ages. Mama has told me that it's very difficult for non-Jews to visit Jews now without risking their own safety and maybe even their lives. But I miss Uldis so much that my stomach hurts and I don't want him ever to see me in the same way that Velna and Helena do.

Dirty Jew.

Mama gets up very deliberately as if it is a superhuman effort to move in the face of my outburst. She picks up my jacket from the floor and hangs it on the back of my bedroom door.

As she does this I see with a jolt that my suitcase is down from the top of my wardrobe and waiting at the end of my bed.

"What's that doing there?" I say. My heart is lurching. For one crazy moment I think that Mama is evicting me from the apartment for staying out too long. But then as I look out into the tiny hallway I see Mama's small red suitcase packed by the front door along with Omama's black one.

"We are leaving," says Mama. "I do not want us to move into the Jewish ghetto. There will not be enough food. Besides, it is in the Maskavas area of town."

I shudder. So they are making us a ghetto, just like in Poland.

The rumours turned out to be true.

I know the Maskavas area. That is the place where all the poor Russians live. Their houses are run-down and basic and look like they are made of slatted cardboard. The houses there have no proper heating or water supplies.

"But at least we would be together and with other Jews," I say. "That can't be so bad, can it? If we leave and go somewhere else, won't we be in even more danger?"

My head is whirling. All the way back from the park I could only think of how good it would feel to get back to this apartment and to the safety of my family, or what's left of it. Even though it is not as good as our beautiful villa, it is starting to feel a bit like home.

Mama lugs my suitcase into the hall and puts it next to the other two.

"There is no guarantee we would stay together in the ghetto," she says. "And there are rumours that people might be sent further east to camps. We could be split up for good. So Brigita has agreed to take us in. It is good of her. We leave tomorrow night."

And the way she says it leaves no room for argument.

Aunt Brigita is Papa's younger sister.

She still lives near to our old house in the Mežaparks area of town in a pretty villa with a garden and four bedrooms. She is married to Georgs and they have no children, just a selection of horrible miniature dogs with short legs and sharp, abrasive barks.

When Papa was still around he avoided Brigita for most of the time. Even though she was his sister they were as different as black bread and matzo. Papa is gentle, laid-back and charming. Brigita is sharp-tongued, impatient and bossy. Her visits always leave Mama plagued with headaches and exhaustion.

Omama can't stand her and always disappears off somewhere else.

"That bony bird gives me the jitters," is all she says.

Brigita hadn't visited us for ages, but then she was here at night-time with Uncle Georgs just over a week ago. I heard her thin, insistent voice arguing with his deeper one when I was supposed to be asleep in bed. I guess that's when Mama hatched her plan.

My aunt does not much like children. When I am left in a room with her I struggle to know what to say. We sit far apart on the sofa and the silence hangs heavy and slow. I reckon she always wanted Papa to marry a rich Latvian widow rather than a struggling Jewish seamstress with a crazy old mother. She disapproves of me wanting to be a dancer, too.

"How will you find time to look after a family if you have a career?" is what she said last time I tried to share my ambitions with her. Aunt Brigita is obsessed with money. She thinks that women should stay home and men should earn all the money. Georgs earns a good salary at one of the largest banks in Rīga and he has even kept his job throughout the Soviet and Nazi occupations and the nationalization of his workplace. Omama mutters in a dark voice that he is probably in league with all sorts of undesirable political parties but in fact Uncle Georgs is a hard worker and a clever man.

He is also far nicer to me than Aunt Brigita ever is. She

just uses his money to feed the best cuts of meat to her revolting dogs.

And now we are going to live with them all.

The next day is strange.

We are all packed up and so we wear the same clothes we wore yesterday. There is no food left except for a few hard bits of bread so Mama toasts them up and tries to make them more palatable by sprinkling caraway seeds all over them but I still nearly choke on the first mouthful.

I feel like a caged animal cooped up in the flat, so in the afternoon I persuade Mama to let me go for a walk down our street.

Mama is very doubtful after my late arrival home yesterday but in the end she looks at my pale skin and the circles under my eyes and agrees that I should get a breath of fresh air.

"Just up and down this street," she says. "Wear your star and stay off the sidewalks. Ten minutes. If you don't come back by then I will have to come and find you. And, Hanna. Don't tell anybody of our plans. And I mean – *anybody*. Okay?"

"Yes, yes," I mutter. I hate this. It's like being a tiny child who can't be trusted to go anywhere or do anything.

I pull on my black jacket with the yellow star and as usual it makes me feel very Jewish and not like Hanna any more. Then I bolt downstairs and out into the air before Mama has a chance to change her mind.

I walk along the gutter, kicking leaves and staring at my shoes. They are starting to wear thin around the sides and the black leather looks almost grey in places. The shoe shops are not open to Jews now. I don't know when I will get a new pair.

I am so busy glaring at my feet that I nearly die of shock when somebody says my name.

"Hanna!"

I stop.

There is Uldis, handsome as ever in his uniform.

I could melt. I have missed him so much that it's taken on a permanent physical ache, like a stomach upset.

"Oh," I say. "It is really good to see you. But where have you been?"

I feel hot in the face when I say this, but it's true. I *have* missed his smooth blond hair and his blue eyes and broad shoulders.

Uldis gives me a brief peck on the cheek.

"I have missed you too," he says. "It is very risky for me to come and visit you where you live. There are punishments – you know?"

I nod. I do know. I have been hearing horrible stories about people who have risked just that and ended up thrown into the Central Prison.

Uldis looks around and resumes an expression like an empty sheet of paper.

"Where are you going?" he says. "You should not still be in this part of town."

I nod.

"I know, it is not safe," I say. "But don't worry. I will be all right. We have plans..."

I don't finish the sentence. Already I have said too much.

What if Uldis turns out to be like Velna? I always thought I could trust her with my life, but now I know otherwise.

I flush, angry with myself. This is Uldis, my beloved Uldis. I have known him since I was a young child. But Mama's face when she made me promise was as hard as iron and her eyes bore into me like drills. I should not let her down.

Uldis has stopped walking and turned to face me. He puts his hand under my chin and tilts it up so that I can look into his eyes.

"Same old Hanna," he says with a smile. "So impulsive and excited, always full of plans for the future. It is why I love you so much, of course."

My heart leaps into my throat.

What did he just say?

We have never exchanged any declarations of love before.

My chest is thumping hard. I stare deep into those blue eyes, trying to see underneath all the flesh and bone and get right down to the soul, to see if he is speaking the truth.

He stares back with that steady gaze. He reaches down and pushes a stray strand of hair out of my eye.

"Well?" he says. "Aren't you going to say it back to me?"

He is grinning now.

I feel as if I want to sit down. My legs have turned to pulp.

"Oh – yes," I stammer. "I do. Love you, I mean. I have done for ages."

Uldis just carries on staring at me. I love his blue eyes so much that I can't drag my gaze away.

"Good," he whispers. "Hanna. If you are going somewhere, you should tell me. I can't bear not to see you again."

"Okay," I say in a whisper back. Then I feel stupid for whispering, as there is nobody else around.

"So you do have a place to stay?" he continues. "That's

good. You will be well taken care of. Where is it? I could try to visit."

I swallow. Mama's face floats in front of my eyes again, concerned and drawn with fear. She has lost a lot of weight. Maybe if Uldis brings us good food she will feel well again.

"I am not supposed to say," I mutter.

Uldis pulls me to him so that my head is resting on the shoulder of his uniform. I can feel the buttons pressing into my cheek.

I stand there swooning in the sunshine with Uldis's lips on my ear and I am dizzy with confusion. It feels important to hang on to this moment and to hang on to Uldis. I have already lost Papa and dancing and now we are about to lose the apartment too. If I tell him where we are going then at least he can come and see us and maybe as I will be living in a non-Jewish household it will be easier for him to avoid any penalties.

"Okay," I say. "We are going to stay with my Aunt Brigita so that we do not have to live in the ghetto. But please keep it to yourself."

Uldis releases me from the embrace.

"Of course," he says. "Please be careful. These are difficult times. Hanna?"

I am already walking away. My lips are shaking with

the effort of trying to hold back a tide of tears. I almost can't bear to say a proper goodbye to Uldis. It is too painful to consider.

"Yes?" I say.

"Good luck," he says. Then he blows me a kiss from his hand and walks away.

Uncle Georgs comes for us that night.

He enters the apartment with a worried look on his face. He is wearing his brown hat and smart brown jacket and his shoes are as polished as ever. Everything about my uncle is brown, right down to his brown eyes and brown moustache.

Tonight he does not smile.

"I am taking a risk coming here," he mutters. "If you could be quick, Kristina."

Mama gives her brother-in-law a peck on the cheek and nods. She hustles me towards the door of the apartment and then looks at me and stops.

"Hanna, pack your jacket with the star," she says. "Just for tonight we will not wear them."

I shoot her a look of amazement but I do as she says. Neither she nor Omama are wearing their stars.

Mama puts a headscarf over her dark hair and ties

another one over my plaits. She takes Omama's arm and Uncle Georgs picks up two of the cases and gestures at me to take my own.

We shut the door to the apartment. It makes a click behind us, even though Mama is trying to be quiet. There is no noise from other apartments because it is three o'clock in the morning, but Mama tells us to creep down the stairs without a sound.

Outside I sniff the early morning air. It has rained and the gutters are gleaming in the semi-gloom. Uncle Georgs's car is waiting. He throws our cases into the boot, gets into the car and gestures to us to do the same. Mama and I get in the back and Omama is given the front seat as she needs more comfort and legroom.

"If we are stopped," says Mama, "don't speak. Leave it to me. We are a Latvian family coming home from a visit to our papa who is in the hospital. Okay?"

"Okay," I say. My heart is pounding as Uncle Georgs negotiates the roads and drives us out of the centre of the old town and towards Mežaparks. It feels strange to be going back as guests to the area we used to live in. Mama has told me that I must behave at all times in Aunt Brigita's house.

We pass the acres of green which make up the park and then Uncle Georgs pulls up outside the house I spent a lot of time at when I was little. Same tidy hedge clipped to perfection, same neat white net curtains and smart orange brickwork. This area of Rīga has as yet been left untouched by the Nazis and, in any case, many of the people living here are non-Jews so can go about their daily business as they always have.

It feels like a different world.

My uncle pushes us all up the front path, clutching our bags and muttering under his breath. I notice that his hand is shaking when he puts the key in the door.

He ushers us down the dark hallway and into the kitchen but he does not put on the light.

"Here," he says, opening the refrigerator. "Brigita left you some sandwiches. She knew you would be hungry."

Omama snorts at this but she reaches out and makes a grab for a sandwich.

"Is this meat kosher?" she says, waving the bread underneath my uncle's nose.

My mother sighs.

"Mama, just eat it," she says. "Be grateful to have good food. For once you will have to put your religion aside."

Omama almost snarls at this but the smell of the savoury meat and fresh bread is too much for her and she sinks her false teeth into the sandwich with a series of horrible squelching noises.

We sit at the kitchen table in the gloom in our

headscarves with our bags by our feet and we eat the sandwiches by the faint light of the crescent moon, shining through Brigita's white curtains.

When we have finished, Uncle Georgs makes coffee and passes it round.

We drink in silence. He seems nervous and does not want to talk to us, which is odd because in the old days he did nothing but chat to us about his job and his dogs and his lovely house.

The dogs are shut outside in the shed at the bottom of the garden. Uncle Georgs says he didn't want them making a noise when we arrived.

I guess he just doesn't want to wake up Aunt Brigita. She probably needs all the beauty sleep she can get.

Uncle Georgs looks up at the kitchen clock about a hundred times a minute and waits for us to finish eating and drinking. Then he takes the plates and cups, washes them up straight away and replaces them all in the cupboard.

I don't remember my uncle being very interested in cleaning the kitchen before. Then I realize. I think he's trying to get rid of the tiniest trace of me, Mama and Omama.

"I could have done that, Uncle," I say. "We must help out while we are here. It is very kind of you to let us stay for a while so that we don't have to move into the ghetto."

My uncle turns round from the sink where he is washing around the plughole with a cloth and some spray and gives Mama a searching look, or at least I think he does. It's hard to tell in the gloom of the unlit kitchen. My eyes are starting to droop with tiredness and I could do with being shown my bedroom.

"You haven't told her the whole story, Kristina?" he says.

Mama shakes her head in silence.

"What do you take us for?" says Omama. "If we had told her that bit, she might have kicked up more of a fuss."

I look from one to the other of them in frustration. Everybody seems to talk in riddles these days. I'm nearly sixteen, not five.

"Told me what?" I say. "Please just be honest. I am too tired for games."

Uncle Georgs gives a laugh when I say this. It is not a friendly laugh but more like the snort of an impatient horse.

"That's a shame," he says. "It would help if you liked games, especially hide-and-seek."

"What?" I say. I am starting to get a sour feeling in my stomach.

Uncle Georgs holds out his hand to me. He is relenting already. I can tell by the way he squeezes my hand and sighs.

"Come with me, petal," he says. "I will show you your room."

He pulls me up a flight of carpeted stairs and onto the landing where I know the bedrooms are.

"Will I have to share with Mama?" I say. I can't remember how many spare rooms the house has.

"Oh yes," says Uncle Georgs. "I am afraid so."

I wait for him to open the door of one of the nice bedrooms with their cosy white beds and pretty floral wallpaper. Instead he surprises me. He moves a set of shelves away from the wall and reveals a small door.

Behind the door is a tiny square patch of carpeted landing and nothing else.

My uncle reaches into a corner and pulls out a long stick.

He hooks the end of the stick into the ceiling and pulls down a hidden hatch. There is a silver ladder folded at one end and he tugs at this until the ladder is folded right out and resting on the floor by my feet.

I look at him and then back at the ladder. Maybe my uncle is playing a joke with me. He doesn't look as if he is finding it very funny, though. In fact even though it is dark I swear I can see that his eyes are shining with tears.

A spider drops through the hatch and hits my face. I scream and brush it off.

"After you," my uncle says, pointing at the ladder. "Welcome to your new home."

Chapter Nine

The first night in our new home does not go well.

Uncle Georgs has put three camp beds up under the low attic beams and several times I sit up in the night in a panic and hit my head.

Up here it is stuffy and warm and we are not allowed to open the windows in case we draw attention to the attic. Uncle Georgs has fitted a pair of thick, dark curtains to shield us from view. I lie on my lumpy mattress and sweat for most of the night.

My room-mates are not the quietest either.

Mama sighs and fidgets in her sleep.

Omama snores and coughs and mutters angry-sounding words.

All in all I get about one hour of sleep.

The three of us struggle up into sitting positions and

open our suitcases to find clean clothes.

"I could do with a wash," says Mama. "I hope Georgs brings us up some water."

My uncle pushes up the hatch, right on cue, and passes a bowl of water up. Then he disappears for a moment, grunting with effort as he descends the ladder. His next appearance yields a tray full of rolls, jam and coffee.

Omama's face lights up a little at this.

"God bless you," she says to my uncle. He gives a faint smile. It doesn't look as if he got much sleep either.

"Is Brigita going to honour us with a visit?" says Mama. "I would like to see my sister-in-law, particularly as I am hiding in her house."

Uncle Georgs sighs. He glances at me, in that annoying way which adults have when they are not sure that they should say something in front of me.

I busy myself splashing water on my face from the white china bowl.

"Hold on," he says. He heaves himself up through the hatch and comes to stand stooped in the middle of the floor.

"Brigita was not keen on the idea of you coming here," says my uncle. "It was I who insisted. Niklas was a good man."

Niklas is Papa.

"Why are you speaking about him as if he is no longer alive?" I say, panic rising in my chest. "He is in Russia. He will come back when the war is over!"

More looks pass between the adults. I wish they wouldn't do this. Do they think that I am blind?

My blindness is starting to lift a little. The more I see what is happening at the hands of the Nazis, the more I have been worrying about what has happened to Papa at the hands of the Soviets. I never realized that people could be capable of such horrors. And I keep wondering why we haven't heard anything from him. Not even a line in a letter or a rumour from someone who might know him.

I know that Papa would try to contact us if he could.

Mama pats my arm and gives me a reassuring smile. Then she helps Omama into her skirt and blouse.

"I'm sorry, Hanna," says my uncle, sitting down on the edge of my bed. "It was just a figure of speech. All I meant was that you are family. Your papa would want me to help you."

That's true. Papa and Uncle Georgs always did get on, in a pipe-smoking sort of a way. The two of them spent hours walking up and down the gravel terrace of our old villa, puffing out clouds of choking smoke and discussing business.

"Can we come downstairs?" I say. The low ceilings and

heat of the attic room are making me feel claustrophobic. “We could make you breakfast.”

Uncle Georgs gives an apologetic smile.

“We think it better that you stay up here for the time being,” he says. “Although I would love you to be downstairs with us, Brigita is very nervous. We have thin walls in this house and our neighbours can hear our voices.”

I remember the middle-aged couple who used to chat to me over the wall in the front garden when I visited as a little girl. They seemed pleasant enough.

“Yes,” says Georgs, reading my mind. “They are nice. But we do not know their feelings about Jews. So it is best to be cautious.”

I nod. First Velna, then some of our old neighbours and now these people who knew me as a little girl and gave me biscuits over the fence. So many people are starting to turn against us.

I stare at Uncle Georgs, hard. He does not look the sort of person who is going to break his word and suddenly hand us in to the police. He would not go to all this trouble unless he was on our side. But how do we trust anybody completely ever again?

“I must show you something now,” he is saying.

He gets up and goes over to the larger of the two windows in the attic roof. He wrenches it open, to my delight. I run over and take a deep breath of the air but he pushes me back and I fall onto my bottom on the hard floor.

"This is only in an emergency," he hisses. "There is a balcony here. If you get onto the balcony you can climb onto the roof."

I stand up and rub my sore behind.

"But why would we want to?" I say. He is not making sense.

My uncle shuts the window and comes back to sit beside me.

He points to a cable on the wall next to my bed. I hadn't noticed it before. The cable ends in a tiny round grey metal object.

"If the Gestapo come looking," he says. "We will try our best to stall them. The loft hatch is as hidden as we can make it. But if we think they are going to move the shelves and enter the attic we will ring from below and this bell will make a noise. Then you have time to get out of the window and onto the roof. After that we cannot help you."

I'm in the middle of cutting open one of the soft breakfast rolls but when Uncle Georgs says the last bit I put it down uneaten. Something about his voice seems to pave the way ahead for us with sharp rocks and falling stones. The Gestapo are the Nazi police, or so Omama has told me.

Mama sees my face and starts to pour coffee into the three tiny rose-patterned cups on the tray.

"This is all so good of you, Georgs," she says. "I am sure we will be very happy and safe in our new temporary home. And please tell Brigita to come up here so that I can thank her too."

My uncle shrugs.

"I will try," he says. "But as I say. She is very frightened of the penalties."

Mama and I nod our understanding as Uncle Georgs begins his grunting descent down the ladder. We have read the threats in *Tēvija* about what happens to Latvian civilians who try to hide or help Jews.

We hear him reach the bottom and then the ladder clangs up and the hatch snaps shut. Beads of sweat have formed on Omama's top lip.

We are stuck up here in the airless attic.

"How long do we have to stay here?" I say. "It won't be for too long, will it?"

Mama sighs.

"Until the war is over," she says. "I am sure it can't be too long now. But we must do as Georgs says and try to bear it with good grace."

I should be hungry. But the rolls may as well be made of lead.

Mama says that if we stick to a routine, we will find it easier.

So, over the next few days she implements the new routine and the three of us try to stick to it. It is not easy. The heat up here is stifling and the lack of exercise and fresh air makes all of us cranky and anxious. I want to ask Uncle Georgs to find out from the outside world how much longer we will have to live like this but Mama has forbidden me to bother him with questions.

"He is bringing food and drink to us," she says. "He is risking his life and Brigita's too. We must remain grateful in our hearts, Hanna. Don't forget that."

I try, but it's not easy to feel grateful when you've got bruises on your skull from bashing it on the beams several times in the day and night. It's not easy when you have to pee into a shared bucket and pass it to your uncle down a small hatch, trying not to splash him with warm yellow urine. It's not easy when it is too hot to sleep and your grandmother snorts and snores within about a metre of you.

The worst thing of all is that I have no space to dance.

I try, but the beams on the ceiling are too low for me to stand upright anywhere other than the centre of the room and there is very little floor space there. So I sit on the edge of my bed with my ballet shoes on and do leg exercises to keep my muscles flexible instead.

Sometimes I get out of bed in the night and risk a peek out of the window. There are few people on the streets around here at that time. This area is still full of wealthy Latvians who go about their daily business as if nothing were happening on the other side of town. It is so different from old Rīga with the ruined church spires and the piles of smouldering rubble and the constant shootings and parading up and down of soldiers and carloads of SS officers.

I should be comforted by the peace and safety in the house but I hate the quiet. It is making me nervous. It is making me wonder what will happen next. The three of us seem suspended away from real life, up here in the attic. We have ceased to be members of the public. We do not have to wear our yellow stars in hiding but that has made me feel even less real.

Mama's routine involves getting up early in the morning even though there is no need. We then say prayers. This is more Omama's idea than Mama's but there is something comforting about the ancient Hebrew words, muttered

-ry softly over a candle that Uncle Georgs has given us on the understanding that we only light it in daylight and on the floor so that there are no reflections outside.

After prayers we eat the breakfast that Georgs brings up every morning.

Sometimes there are fresh rolls and coffee but at other times there is a loaf of harder bread and a jug of water. Uncle Georgs says that food supplies are running short even for Latvians but I reckon Aunt Brigita wants to keep the best stuff for herself. When I say this to Mama she slaps my wrist and tells me to keep my uncharitable thoughts to myself, but I still think I'm right. We have been here for two weeks now and my aunt hasn't once even bothered to come and say hello.

When breakfast is finished Mama gets me to make up all three camp beds. I do it even though I bang my head.

Uncle Georgs brings up the morning paper just after eleven and Omama settles down on her bed to read it. Mama has all her cottons and wools with her so she often knits or sews for a couple of hours. I am allowed to read one of the books that my uncle has passed up. Most of them are a bit childish and concern horses or dull family sagas but it's less boring than just lying on my bed.

At lunchtime another tray of bread and coffee is passed up. Sometimes there is a little fruit. It tends to be bruised or under-ripe but it is good to have something other tha[n] bread so we eat it.

In the afternoon the heat tends to get so oppressive Omama lies down on her bed and falls fast asleep. Mama tries to read but she too often falls asleep, worn out by heat and worry. Sometimes I join them but most of the time I just lie on my back and stare up at the woodworm-ridden beams over my bed and I think about what I am going to do when I get out of here.

Most of my plans involve Uldis.

I really miss him and think back to when I last saw him. He said he would visit, so I am holding out for that moment but the frustrating thing is that I can't do anything about it stuck up here.

Sometimes when Mama and Omama are asleep I feel a bit hot and flustered thinking about Uldis. I relive our last conversation in painstaking detail, trying to remember exactly what he said and how I responded and whether I came across as mature and romantic or a bit silly and I remember what it was like to kiss him properly in the dark back row of the Rīga cinema before the Nazis came. Then a reality check slaps me round the face like a wet salmon and I remember that Jews are no longer allowed to go to the cinema and I replay the look on Velna's face and hear the spiteful laugh of Marija Otis right up close to my ear.

It is nice to remember all the things that Uldis has said to me, though. I feel sure that he will honour his word and bring us food when he can, but thinking about him makes me feel hot and funny and a bit frustrated and the walls seem to close in on me. I am always relieved and half-glad when Mama rubs the sleep out of her eyes and yawns and says that perhaps we should play a board game before supper.

The game kills the final few dull hours of stupefying heat and boredom and Uncle Georgs is visibly relieved to be handing us our last tray of the evening.

"Goodnight," he whispers as he descends the ladder and clangs us back inside our hot prison.

We eat the soup that he has brought us and if it is the Sabbath, say our special Friday night prayers.

Mama's routine seems to keep us calm.

We have been up in Uncle Georgs's attic for just over a month.

By now we no longer complain or argue much. Georgs has urged us to keep our voices down.

One evening we have a reminder of why we are hiding.

We are laughing in low murmurs over our board game and then we hear the doorbell go downstairs and the sound of Uncle Georgs's two dogs barking. We freeze. Usually it is a friend or neighbour of Uncle Georgs but something about the way in which this sound goes on for a fraction longer than usual makes us glance at one another and then sweep the game under one of the beds.

Mama goes over to the window and clicks it open as softly as she can. The three of us stand by the window in our coats even though it is boiling. I can barely find enough breath in my body to keep from falling over.

There are harsh voices downstairs. Men's voices, loaded with authority and disrespect. I can hear Uncle Georgs protesting at something and then the hysterical chirp of Aunt Brigita's voice, which is the only bit of her I ever hear, cutting into what her husband is saying.

Then we hear it.

Footsteps, pounding up the stairs towards the first floor.

It sounds like at least two men, possibly more.

All we can do is stand huddled by the window, staring at the circular grey bell on the wall.

"Why doesn't he ring it?" I whisper.

Mama flashes her eyes at me. It means "be quiet".

I strain to hear.

I am listening for the sound of those shelves being pushed back to reveal the hidden loft hatch. I know the aping sound it makes because I hear Uncle Georgs do it very time he comes to see us.

I strain so hard that I can hear blood rushing around inside my head.

Nothing.

The footsteps seem to be running in and out of the first-floor bedrooms.

Then they pound downstairs again and we hear the front door being opened and Uncle Georgs saying something in a polite voice.

The door shuts.

Then the yelling begins.

Aunt Brigita screams at my uncle all evening.

I feel sick, hearing the hysterical tone of her voice go on and on at kind Uncle Georgs.

He tells her to be quiet.

"They will hear you!" he says. "And so will half the neighbourhood. Be quiet, woman, unless you want all of us to end up in the Central Prison!"

There's a stunned silence and then the sound of my aunt storming upstairs. But instead of going to her bedroom and slamming the door, we hear the sound of the shelf being dragged aside in a frenzy. There's a loud

bang on the loft hatch and a curse as the ladder falls do
out of control.

The sound of hard-soled shoes clicking up the metal ladder then the face of my aunt appears through the hatch.

Mama is very composed. I admire her at times like this. You would think from her calm tone of voice that she was greeting Aunt Brigita at a party, rather than in a poky hot loft which my aunt has managed to avoid for a month now.

"Why, hello Brigita!" she says. "How lovely to see you. I was so hoping that you would be kind enough to come and visit us."

This takes the wind out of Aunt Brigita's puffed-up sails. She never did know what to make of my mother.

Her face is very red and pinched, though. And her grey hair is shoved up into a prim bun. With her thick-rimmed black spectacles she reminds me of a teacher I used to hate at school.

"Hello, Aunt," I say in a subdued voice. Brigita doesn't even look at me, or at Omama who is glaring at her from her bed in the corner.

"I hope you are satisfied," she says in a high, trembling voice. "We have had the Gestapo here tonight."

"Yes," says Mama in a mild tone. "I thought I heard them."

"We could all have been shot," says my aunt. Her hands on the floor of the loft are shaking. "It was not my idea that you came here. We must all suffer because of you."

"Uh-huh," says Mama in that strange, neutral voice. "Even though we are the family of your own dear brother."

Aunt Brigita flushes a deeper shade of purple.

"He made his choice when he married you," she says. "It is not my fault that my brother turned out to be so stupid."

Mama stares at her sister-in-law in astonishment. I'm doing the same. Although she's always been a bit snippy she used to manage to be polite to us. Now it's like that veneer has been stripped away to reveal a deep hatred underneath.

We are getting used to being hated, but not by our own family. I feel sick to the pit of my stomach. Is there nobody who likes us any more? What have we ever done to these people except invite them to sit at Mama's table and eat our lovely food?

I can see Mama struggling for words but she needn't have bothered.

Omama has pushed herself up into a bent walking position and is standing above the hatch and glaring down at my aunt.

"You bitter, shrew-faced old misery," she says. I hide my face behind my pillow. When Omama gets going there's no stopping her.

"What do you know about suffering?" continues Omama. "Here in your fancy house with all your expensive things and your silly clothing and your husband who works hard to give you what you want."

Aunt Brigita has started to descend the ladder but Omama reaches down with her walking stick and grabs a lapel of her white silk blouse.

"May God have mercy on you," she hisses. "And teach you some compassion, for His sake."

Then she makes a stabbing motion with the stick and Aunt Brigita practically jumps the last few rungs of the ladder onto the safety of the carpeted landing.

We hear her bedroom door slam and then there is silence.

"Well," says Mama. She shuts the hatch and sits down so hard that I hear a bedspring snap. Her face is very pale. "That told her, Mama. But maybe you should tone it down a little in future? We are guests in her house, after all!"

Omama snorts and gives her big Jewish Grandmother shrug. Then she winks at me.

"We might lose everything else, but we still have our pride, eh?" she says.

I smile back but I feel sick and shaky and wracked with worry.

My heart is pounding.

Aunt Brigita will not let us stay here much longer.

It looks as if even our own family will turn against us soon.

So what will happen to us then?

Chapter Ten

AFTER THE VISIT FROM AUNT BRIGITA we wait in fear for Uncle Georgs to come up and tell us that we must leave his house.

Mama says that we could go back to our apartment in the old town and hide up in the attics of the building, but we know that this would not be ideal. There are too many other non-Jews in the apartment block and they would hear us moving around overhead.

Omama reckons that her Rabbi might be able to help us, but this would mean leaving the suburbs and somehow going into town to look for him, so that's too risky.

"Maybe we should just move to the ghetto," I say, trying to help.

Mama's face becomes pinched and stubborn.

"No," she says. "I will not move there. Not to that district. We are better off up here but only if Uncle Georgs agrees to let us stay."

We are silent for a moment. Last night very late we heard Georgs and Brigita have another whispered argument in their bedroom below our feet.

And last night for the first time, Georgs did not bring us any supper on a tray.

It makes me feel sick with guilt that their marriage is in trouble because of us, even though I don't much like my aunt.

There is nothing we can do this morning except wait.

It is our Jewish New Year today.

It falls at the end of September and its real name is Rosh Hashanah.

If we had been at home and not holed up in an attic with no table or cooking facilities we would have started the celebrations at sunset after the ram's horn had been blown at synagogue to symbolize the sobbing and wailing of Abraham offering his son to God. The celebration would have gone on for two days.

However it's a bit difficult to do anything much without any food up here and I don't fancy our chances blowing any sort of horn with the Aunt Brigita Police on duty downstairs.

So we wish each other a Happy New Year with kisses and hugs and try hard not to see the irony in our wishes.

Omama pinches my cheek in that special way that she has and my eyes water with pain but I kiss her anyway.

Then we sit on the edges of our beds and wait.

At ten o'clock, Uncle Georgs burst through the loft hatch.

He is smiling and a little out of breath.

He gestures at me to take the tray and I cry out when I see it.

There is a round shiny challah and a jar of honey.

"I made it in the middle of the night when I couldn't sleep," he says, going a little pink. "I remembered that it was today."

Mama comes over and plants a big kiss on the top of Georgs's head.

"Oh, you are a good man," she says. "A thousand thanks. This will make our day special."

Uncle Georgs clears his throat and starts to descend the ladder, but then he comes up again as if he's just remembered something.

"I have had words with my wife," he says. "Don't worry. You can stay here as long as it takes. Happy New Year!"

He goes down and we hear the shelves being slid into place.

Mama sits on her bed and bursts into tears.

We eat the shiny challah, dipping the sweet pieces into the sticky honey and cramming it into our mouths. We are not supposed to have it until the evening but up here the rules are bent so much every day that even Omama doesn't really mind.

"We dip this bread into honey so that the forthcoming year will be sweet," she says, honey running down her chin. "And we eat the round challah also so that the year will be rounded, like a circle."

Mama gives a very un-Mama-like snort.

"How will it be?" is all she says, but the bread doesn't taste so good after that. I know that she's right, but sometimes I just want to pretend everything is going to be okay.

I make a big fuss of pulling off more challah and dipping it into the divine honey.

We do not eat as much here as we would like to, so to

have a whole loaf and a jar of honey makes me feel rich for the entire morning. And there is fresh coffee, too. Uncle Georgs has gone all out to try and make our New Year special.

And he has more surprises in store.

By the late afternoon Omama is trawling through the papers and Mama is asleep on her bed as usual. There is a gentle click and Uncle Georgs appears with our supper tray. It is earlier than usual so I am surprised.

He slides the tray onto the floor and beckons me over.

"A special supper," he says. "I had to assemble it while Brigita was at her reading circle. She is not to know I spent money on this. Happy New Year!"

My brilliant uncle disappears down the hatch and I stare at the tray.

There is a steaming dish of chicken soup with little white noodles floating in the golden liquid. Next to it is a platter with a whole fish on. We eat a whole fish at Rosh Hashanah to symbolize fertility. And under a cloth on another plate is a golden square of apple strudel, stuffed with plump raisins and fat wedges of sugary apple. There are white china plates and silvery cutlery.

And a glass carafe containing red wine.

"Mama," I whisper. "Wake up."

My mother struggles into a sitting position and tries

to focus her tired eyes on the tray. When she does, she claps her hands without making a sound and hugs me to her.

Omama is already slurping the soup.

It is the best evening we have had since we moved into this attic over a month ago.

For one evening we forget that we are all a little thinner and paler from lack of balanced meals and fresh air. We forget about Omama's worsening hip and the way that all my ballet muscles are less defined even though I try to run through a set of exercises whenever I can. We forget that we are homeless and do not know what lies ahead of us.

There is only one thing we do not forget. Well – one person.

"To Papa," I say, raising the small glass of wine that Mama has allowed me.

"To Papa," says Mama, her eyes glistening. "And to dear, dear Uncle Georgs."

I think of Uldis with a pang in my stomach. I miss him so much, stuck up here away from the rest of the world.

We clink glasses very softly and smile at one another.

So the first day of our Rosh Hashanah is everything we could have wished for and more.

We do not get to observe the second.

At one o'clock in the morning we are woken from our wine-drenched sleep by a banging noise.

"Quick," says Mama, wide awake in seconds. "Onto the balcony, Hanna."

I start to open the window as softly as I can.

Mama helps Omama on with her coat and herds us both underneath the window.

The night air comes through the cracks. It is sharp and acidic. There is some sort of danger in the air, like gunpowder.

I start to shiver. The three of us stare at the grey bell. I pray hard for it not to go off.

When it does, I jump so hard that I bang my elbow against the window frame.

"Go," says Mama.

Just one word, but we know what we have to do.

I push open the window and climb onto the balcony.

Then I lean back in to give Mama my hand. I help her out and then between us we manage to haul Omama out by her arms. It is a good job she is so skinny.

Mama shuts the window behind us and looks up at the roof.

"Climb up as far as you can towards the middle," she hisses. "Stay very still when you get there. I will be right behind you."

I begin to climb up the roof in my shoes and nightdress but then I look down at Mama and Omama standing there looking up at me and my heart contracts.

I promised Papa I'd look after them.

I slither back down the roof tiles backwards and my feet hit the balcony.

"Hanna," says Mama. "What are you doing? Get back on the roof at once!"

"You and Omama go up first," I say. "I will help you."

There is no time for argument. With an anguished look at me, Mama climbs onto the roof tiles and turns around to extend her hand to Omama.

Omama reaches up a skinny wrist and grabs Mama's hand. I push her legs up and between us, Mama and I try to heave Omama onto the roof but it is no good. Her sore hip and her skinny legs are a lethal combination. Her legs slip and slide as they try to find footing on the black slates and a great tile comes loose.

It crashes to the ground below and smashes into pieces. The noise may as well be a cannon shot.

"Well, that's us done for. Perhaps we should have practised?" says Omama. She is back on the balcony.

I laugh. I am surprised that Omama can still be so funny in this situation.

Mama hesitates on the roof. Then she slides back down again.

And that is where they find the three of us.

Cold, defiant, huddled together on a tiny balcony in our coats and nightdresses.

The two Gestapo men, standing with their guns and their snarling, pulling dogs.

And behind them, in his yellow-green uniform with the red striped armband and wearing an expression of something that I can't read...

Uldis.

Chapter Eleven

THE DOGS BARK, THICK SNOUTS pointing up towards the night sky and fat bodies straining at their black leather leashes.

Downstairs Uncle Georgs's dogs are going crazy.

One of the Gestapo men shouts at the dogs and they whimper and settle down at his feet.

I am shivering hard. It is not cold outside but inside I am full of rising fear. I can't stop staring at Uldis. There has been some mistake. Why will he not look at me? I cling onto Mama's arm on one side and Omama's on the other. Omama's arm feels like the bone in the middle of a shank of lamb but without all the meat and fat clinging to it.

Then it hits me as hard as if I had been attacked with the butt of a rifle.

This is because of me.

I told Uldis where we were hiding.

I have betrayed my own family.

"Name?" says the man who has shouted at the dogs.

Mama steps forward off the balcony and climbs back through the window, gesturing at us to follow. Her head is held high and I recognize the determined lift of her chin. My mother is a proud woman.

"Kristina Michelson," she says. "This is my mother Ita Dzintra and my daughter Hanna Michelson."

I shoot Omama a look of astonishment.

"I did not know that was your name," I whisper.

Omama shrugs.

"What can I say?" she answers. "I am an enigma."

Then she pinches my cheek very hard. The tears that this brings are added to the tears I already have in my eyes. Everything I love and have left in the world is huddled here in a poky room in front of the Gestapo and their vile dogs. The world has shrunk right down to this attic and this moment.

"Michelson, huh?" says the man. He comes over and looks straight down into my face.

I try and stare back with as much impudence as I can muster, but my arms and legs and head are shaking. I can't seem to look at Uldis and his face is in shadow in the dark corner of our attic. But his stance – folded arms, unmoving – is telling me things I don't want to know.

"Jew?" says the man. "But you are not wearing your star."

In the panic to get outside I forgot to put on my jacket with the star sewn on.

Mama pushes me behind her and steps up to the man. She only reaches the level of his chin but she can be very intimidating when she gets going.

"We were sleeping!" she says. "You expect us to wear the star when we are asleep?"

The man looks at his colleague and exchanges one of those vile, lazy smiles.

"What shall we do with these Jews?" he says. "They are very bolshie."

Mama stares him straight in the eye.

"You can do what you want with me," she says. "Yes. I am a Jew, and proud of it. But I ask you to spare my mother as she is old. And my daughter is only a half-Jew."

The man and his colleague share another smile.

Then he pushes my mother out of the way so that she stumbles against Omama. He lifts my chin and looks straight at me.

"*Mischlinge*," he says. "Aryan blood contaminated by a Jew!"

Then he spits straight into my face.

All this time Uldis has stood at the back of the attic room, stooped over to avoid banging his head on the beams.

My thoughts are all over the place.

How could you hate me this much? What have I ever done to you other than shower you with love and want to spend time with you?

My anger is rising up in a red mist in front of my eyes.

At that moment there's a slight bang downstairs. I recognize the sound of Uncle Georgs's front door. I half turn my head and see my uncle and aunt scurrying down the front path like frightened mice, carrying their leather suitcases and wearing hats and coats.

In a heartbeat both the Gestapo men have thrown themselves down the loft hatch, snapping instructions at Uldis on their way down.

We hear them burst out of the front door and shout a one-word order at Georgs and Brigita, who are at the front wheel of their car. The dogs are let loose and stand in front of the car, barking their harsh, repetitive warning. I watch my aunt and uncle getting out of the car and trying to fend them off.

There's a commotion of shouting and confusion and I hear my aunt's scream and my uncle's voice raised in protest.

Then there is a shot.

Then another.

"Mother of God," cries Mama. "No. Please no."

Even Omama looks scared. I have never seen that haunted look in her eyes before. Now she looks just like what she is – a tiny, bent-over old lady who is weak from lack of proper food and emaciated by old age and worry. It's like her big personality has been sucked out of the attic and flown over the rooftops seeking another home in the city.

"Mama," I whimper, "what are they going to do to us?"

My mother looks at Uldis. All this time he has been standing silent in the attic, although I notice he has brought his gun out of its holster and is now holding it with some awkwardness, like an angular newborn baby.

"Perhaps you can tell us," she says. Her voice is cold and thin. "I knew that you had volunteered. I knew about your father. But I was hoping you had more sense, Uldis. Your mother is a good woman and for her sake I've allowed you into our lives against my better judgement. Why are you hunting down innocent people? Where is your pride?"

Uldis steps out from the shadows in the eaves. His face betrays no emotion under his peaked cap. The blue eyes which I have always loved seem to have lost their clarity and taken on a dull, glazed look.

"How did you find us?" says Omama with a spark of her old outrage.

"Hanna told me you were hiding here," he says. Mama and Omama both gasp at this. They look at me for confirmation. I give a small, ashamed nod.

"Hanna," says Mama, "how could you? I told you to tell nobody of our plans. Nobody."

I flush with fear and anger.

"I thought Uldis was different," I say. "He told me he loved me."

"Oh, Hanna," sighs Mama. "No. You have been fooled."

This is all too much to take in. Only months ago I was going to the cinema with Uldis and even though I had decided to put my ballet career above everything, I still had a dream of marrying him and having lots of blue-eyed, blond-haired children who looked a little like both of us.

Now he is standing here with that strange, detached look in his eyes and I feel as if I am in a waking nightmare.

"So?" says Omama, shuffling forward to peer up at Uldis. "What have you got to say for yourself? Why pick on us? What have we ever done to you, other than welcome you into our home and give you our food?"

A sneer settles on Uldis's thin face.

"You are Jews," he says. "Responsible for everything bad in this country. I am helping Herr Hitler cleanse Latvia of your race."

Neither Mama or Omama look surprised at what he says, but my spine goes cold.

"But you told me you loved me..." I begin, but we are interrupted by one of the Gestapo, who bursts back into the attic and orders us downstairs.

He has his gun in my back.

I guess he thinks I'm the most likely to make a run for it. I'm the youngest and fittest out of the three of us. But I can never leave Mama and Omama. I promised Papa and I am not the sort of girl who breaks an important promise.

So I let him shove me downstairs towards the armoured vehicle revved up outside. The other Gestapo man is already at the wheel, drinking out of a bottle and staring straight ahead like he's tired of us already.

The front path is littered with the clothes from Uncle Georgs's suitcase. I step over shirts and hats and trousers and then I stop. My aunt and uncle are lying motionless amidst the piles of clothing. Uncle Georgs's left leg in its brown trouser is bent out at a strange angle, like a stork. I can see my aunt's face. She is staring up at the sky with her red-lipped mouth opened in a half-circle, like she is about to sing.

A patch of dark red seeps into the cracks in the pavement and spreads out like a jagged fan.

"Move forward," hisses the second Gestapo man.

I stumble over the bodies and get into the car, weeping. I daren't look round to see if Mama and Omama are coming but inside my head I pray to God for them to stay alive.

I hear Mama's scream of shock as she treads the same route and I hear her consoling Omama over and over in a low voice. They are both pushed into the back seat with me.

The vehicle roars away from my aunt and uncle's house.

I clasp the hands of my mother and grandmother and look at the back of Uldis's head. He is sitting in the front seat with the two men and he betrays no emotion at all. They pass him the bottle and he takes a swig. I get a whiff of the sharp, sterile smell of vodka.

I am horrified and in shock because of what has happened to my kind uncle and his wife and I am sickened to the core by Uldis's betrayal, but there is a worse emotion bubbling up and threatening to overtake all others.

Guilt.

I sit and shake in silence, tears running down my face and dropping onto my hands.

All I can think during the short journey back towards town is:

Why, Uldis? Why did you betray us? What did we ever do to you?

But worse that that, I know that this has all happened because of me.

Chapter Twelve

We are driven back into the Vecrīga district.

My heart contracts as I see the familiar burned-out shell of St Peter's Church and the jagged remains of the Great Choral Synagogue. We pass my first school, now boarded-up and vandalized and the Freedom Monument, which is under heavy armed guard, and then the car passes the white *Opera* nearby in the park by the narrow canal.

I stare through the glass at this building where I had planned to take the ballet world by storm some day and I realize that there may as well be a pane of glass between me and my city of dreaming spires for ever.

Although Uldis is sitting so close in front of me that I could touch his head if I wanted to, it's as if we are in separate countries. The love between us has been sucked away and replaced by something else – shock, on my part. Hatred on his.

Mama is sniffing next to me. I pull out a handkerchief from my pocket and give it to her, only it's not a handkerchief but the spare yellow star that Mama forced me to keep in my pocket in case one of my others came loose.

She shoves it up her own sleeve with a horrified look. God only knows what the Gestapo would do to us if they saw us using the star to blow our dripping noses!

So Mama sniffs until we pull up outside a building.

We are astonished.

It is our apartment building.

We stare at one another, not comprehending. Then the driver gets out and pulls open the back door. He gestures us into the gutter. We have no luggage – that was all left at Uncle Georgs's house in the panic to obey orders – so it is just the three of us standing huddled together again in front of our old home.

"As you have not tried to run," says the man in his charming voice, as if he were speaking to his favourite sisters, "we are not going to shoot you. You have until dawn to get your belongings and move into the ghetto."

"Oh," says Mama. "Thank you. Thank you for sparing our lives."

She reaches out her hand to shake his.

He gives a sharp laugh and takes a step backwards.

"It is not a favour," he says. "You Jews will get what's coming to you."

The skull on his cap glows in the light from the moon.

Then he gets back into the car. All this time Uldis remains in the front seat. He does not even turn round to see where we are going.

The car roars off into the night.

"Come on, Hanna," says Mama. I have fallen to my knees in the street, sobbing. I feel as if my life has ended. I have lost Uldis and somehow managed to betray my beautiful mother and my crazy old grandmother too and now because of my stupid actions kind Uncle Georgs and frightened Aunt Brigita have been shot dead.

Mama helps me up on one side and Omama pulls me up on the other. "He is not worth it," says Mama. "We have other problems now."

We go upstairs and back into our apartment.

There is no need to find a key for the door.

The rooms have already been looted.

The living room has had most of the furniture removed and the few bits left are broken and tossed about like boat wreckage after a storm in a small harbour.

The curtains have been pulled down and one of the windows smashed so that the broken glass resembles a snowflake. A draught blows through the apartment.

Omama goes straight into her tiny bedroom and we hear her muttering and moving stuff about. Then there is a crow of delight. She heads back into the living room clutching something to her chest.

"Mama!" says my mother, outraged. "You surely didn't leave that here? We could have all been shot if the police had seen it!"

"Well they didn't," says Omama in triumph. She is clutching the small black square and almost dancing round in circles of joy, though because of her stiff hip it is more like watching a lurching walrus.

It is her radio. Somehow Omama has found a place to hide it and it is still intact and working, judging by the crackling noises coming from inside.

"Switch that off!" hisses Mama. "For God's sake. We are not even supposed to be here. Say whoever trashed this apartment decides to come back? Possession of a radio is illegal, Mama."

Omama pulls a face like a sulky child. Then she winks at me and shoves the radio inside the waistband of her skirt.

Mama gives a heavy sigh but she is already looking around for things that we can still use.

"We need to pack," she says. "It is nearly dawn. We must move to the ghetto. Just what I did not want to happen. At least we will find our friends there."

I start to help her in a daze. All I can see is the hard, cold expression on Uldis's face and the way he looked at us as if we were pieces of dirt on his polished shoe. How can this be the same person who told me he loved me and put his arm around me at the cinema? I feel dizzy, as if somebody has taken away all the support from my life and left me wobbling unaided in the middle. When I'm not seeing Uldis's face I see the sprawled dead bodies of my aunt and uncle lying bent and broken on their front path and it makes me shake inside so that I can't stand still.

I don't even really know what a ghetto is. All I have managed to glean from Mama is that it is in the run-down *Maskavas Forštate* of town where those poor Russians have lived for years in houses without electricity or sometimes even water.

"Why do we have to live in the ghetto?" I say.

Mama snaps the lid shut on her small suitcase.

Omama gives one of her sarcastic snorts.

"Because the Nazis want the streets of Rīga to be *judenrein*," she says.

My stomach gives a little gulp.

Free of Jews. They want to push us out of our own city.

I think of Uldis again.

"Why did Uldis betray us?" I say. "Why did he stand there with a gun? Why does he hate us so much?"

My voice catches on the last word. I've just realized that my life has turned a corner I didn't want it to go round and that there will be no turning back.

Mama and Omama exchange one of their looks. Mama gives a slight nod. Then Omama disappears for a moment and comes back clutching a copy of *Tēvija.*

She passes it to me with a sad smile, tapping at the black print with her bony finger.

The paper is dated 4th July. The same day our Great Choral Synagogue burned down. This is what it says:

In big black font there is an appeal:

All patriotic Latvians, Pērkonkrusts members, students, officers, militiamen, and citizens, who are ready to actively take part in the cleansing of our country of undesirable elements should enrol themselves at the office of the Security Group at 19 Valdemāra iela.

I look from the paper to Mama's anguished face and back again. The words start to rearrange themselves on the page until I am staring at "undesirable elements", which seems blacker than all the other text.

"That's us," I say in a whisper.

"Yes," says Omama. "And your Uldis is one of those 'patriotic Latvians', I am afraid. Like father like son. When you lived next door to them his mother once let slip that Mr Lapa had been a member of Pērkonkrusts back in the 1930s."

I shudder. I have read all about the anti-Semitic Pērkonkrusts political party in *Tēvija.* They were outlawed by the Latvian government in 1934, but their slogan "Latvia for Latvians – Work and bread for Latvians!" is too close to what Uldis once said when I asked him why he was joining the auxiliary police. And yet because I loved him I chose to hear everything he said, and view everything he did, as good.

So he had been planning his betrayal of us since the beginning of July.

I sink down onto the floor as our chairs have been taken.

"Why didn't you tell me?" I whisper.

Mama comes and sits on the floor next to me. She puts her arm around my shoulders and presses herself close to me.

"Uldis's mother is a good woman," she says. "She does not share the beliefs of her husband and son. It was because of her that we let you see Uldis even though I was never really happy with it, as you probably could tell."

"I thought it was because you wanted me to make a Jewish marriage," I say, leaning into her.

Mama laughs.

"Why would I want that?" she says. "I was happy with Papa, no? And he was not a Jew."

I note that she says "was" rather than "am" but I am too tired to protest.

"Besides," says Mama, "we did not think you would ever have to see Uldis again after we went into hiding."

"Well, you got that bit wrong," I say. A new feeling is rising up inside me. Anger. Anger at the way Uldis sat at our family table when Papa was still here and talked about his plans for the future and ate our beautiful home-cooked food and charmed my Omama.

A whole chunk of my future will have to be rewritten. No more blond-haired blue-eyed children with handsome, chisel-faced Uldis.

When I think of him from now on, I will try just to see a rat. Rats are slippery and unpleasant and have eyes that are too close together.

But it will not stop the hurt of his betrayal. I know that. I feel old, weary, about a hundred. It is like I have gone to sleep in a world of fantasy and woken up in a world of real life. In the cold light of day, everything I have left looks fragile and unappealing.

"We need to focus on getting to the Russian part of town now," Mama is saying. "We have to go to the ghetto, Hanna."

"Where will the Russians go?" I say.

I picture us moving into their houses without them leaving. All squashed together and speaking different languages.

"Hanna, there is no time for your questions," says Mama. "See if you can find any plates and spoons in the kitchen. And cups or bowls. I need to sort out transport."

She goes downstairs to the cellar of our apartment building, leaving me and Omama pulling together the few possessions we can find.

Twenty minutes later Mama comes in triumphant with two wheelbarrows and wobbles them sideways to fit them through the front door.

"There," she says. "Now we can move."

I stare at the barrows in disbelief. They are not very big, plus one of them has a broken wheel at the front.

"We have to use these?" I say.

Mama comes over to put her arms around me.

"Hanna," she says, "we are not allowed to have private transportation. We are not allowed to get on trains or buses or boats or hire carriages. We are not even allowed to walk on the sidewalks. So we have to use what we can."

Omama is already putting pillows and blankets into one of the barrows.

"Perhaps we should push you, Mama," says my mother. "You are very thin. I have just found out from the caretaker that there is a *Gesundheitsamt* set up to help those who are elderly or unwell. They can give us a pushcart."

Omama stands up straight and glares at us.

"I might be old," she says, "and yes, my arms and legs do not work as well as they once did. But I've still got enough dignity not to be pushed in front of the population of Rīga in a barrow, thank you very much."

As a last gesture of defiance she chucks the small black radio on top of the pile.

Mama groans.

"At least put a blanket over it!" she says. But she does not offer to put Omama in a pushcart again. Omama seems to have got a bit of her fighting spirit back since we were hustled out of Uncle Georgs's attic.

None of us mention what happened to Uncle Georgs and Aunt Brigita.

It is too raw. We can't yet find the words.

*

We leave our apartment the next morning.

The weather is starting to take on a sharp edge. Mama has spent the rest of the early hours sewing new yellow stars onto our winter coats so that we can wear them over our thinner jackets and, in that way, manage to take as much clothing as we are able into the ghetto.

We have loaded up the two wheelbarrows with blankets, pillows, pots, pans and as many clothes as we can fit in. Mama manages to squeeze her sewing kit in on the very top. We tie the bulky loads down with pieces of rope so that our belongings do not fall out in the street.

The janitor of our apartment block helps us carry both barrows downstairs, although he pulls a face when Mama asks him and says he won't go any further than the downstairs corridor.

"You Jews are nothing but trouble," he says. But his face is not cross when he says this. He's always had a soft spot for Mama. I reckon he's scared, just like the rest of the non-Jewish population of Rīga now. He is risking his life by helping us.

"Thank you," my mother says to him. "We will leave you in peace now."

We stand outside the door to our apartment block and look up at the building one last time.

Then Mama and I push the two barrows into the

gutter and, with Omama walking behind, we start our journey out of the old town and towards our new home.

It takes nearly an hour to navigate our barrows into *Maskavas iela* and the heart of the ghetto.

We struggle across town, alongside the river, and join other streams of Jews pulling carts, wagons and barrows loaded up with their only remaining possessions.

The Latvian citizens of Rīga regard us impassively from behind their coat collars as they hurry to work. Some of them mime things at their Jewish friends on the way past. Others go out of their way to cross the road when they see us coming. Helena and her mother are heading towards the centre of the old town where they will buy food in the shops we are not allowed to queue in and sit in the cafes we are no longer allowed to eat in. Mama risks a wave but is rewarded with a blank, hard stare from the friends she has had for years.

"Told you," I mutter. I don't even try to make eye contact with Helena. What is the point? She will not lower herself to offer a smile to a Jew.

There is a marked contrast between the speed of Rīga's workforce hurrying along in their smart office clothes in one direction and the slow, cumbersome pace of us Jews of Rīga, with our yellow stars visible on coats and jackets dragging our loads in the other.

"Oh," says Mama, her face brightening. "Look. There is Mr Gutkin!"

She is pointing at Rīga's leading manufacturer of our beloved matzo crackers. He is being wheeled along in one of the makeshift pushcarts that Mama wanted to get for Omama. He is waving and smiling at everybody in the Jewish queue as he travels beside them. I like Mr Gutkin's grey moustache and beard and his kind dark eyes.

"Free matzo for everyone after we leave the ghetto!" he is shouting. Many of the Jews are smiling and shouting back, but Omama's face is set like stone.

"He is living in a world of fantasy," she mutters. "Maybe he ate too much of his own damned bread!"

I can tell that Omama's bad temper is because her hip is hurting, but I'm too frightened to stop wheeling my barrow along the uneven gutters so that I can turn round and help her. There are SS units in open-topped cars patrolling up and down the streets and every now and again their soldiers leap out and beat the slow-moving Jews until they either speed up or fall to the ground and lie there motionless.

I dare not stop.

*

On the endless walk we learn from other Jews that we must report to the Jewish Council in *Lāčplēša iela*.

When we reach this street we are cold and numb from lack of sleep the night before.

There is chaos in the large school building which has been converted into the headquarters of the Jewish community. Here a small number of Jewish men and women have been assigned by the Nazis to manage every aspect of our lives in the ghetto.

A dark-haired lady called Mrs Blumenfeld is in charge of the apartment office which deals with housing. She is wearing a white armband with a blue Star of David on it and sitting at a small desk being begged and besieged by several hundred desperate Jews who have walked across town and now have no place to live. In the courtyard at the back of the building, despondent people sit on barrows and suitcases with their heads in their hands whilst their children cling to them and cry.

Mama sits Omama down outside in the courtyard and puts her own coat around Omama's shoulders before she remembers that she can't remove her own yellow star, so she takes it back again and then she and I queue up for nearly two hours until it is our turn to be dealt with.

Mrs Blumenfeld looks up our names and then copies them into a large register.

"You have been assigned a first floor room at number 29, *Ludzas iela*," she says. "There are already some Jews in the building and you will probably have to share the room with others."

I look at Mama, horrified, but Mama is signing her name on a document and appears to have nothing to say about this latest horrid twist of fate.

"Go and register at the labour office across the street," says Mrs Blumenfeld. "All able-bodied Jews must work."

Mama nods. Her face is full of fear and confusion but she is determined not to make a fuss.

Then we negotiate our barrows out of the crowded community centre buildings and with Omama grumbling behind us, enter the crowded building of the labour office at 145 *Lāčplēša*. Mama and I queue up again and are given yellow cards.

"We already have blue cards," says Mama. She means the ones we first got when we registered at the police station for work.

The man behind the desk frowns.

"It says here you are seamstresses," he says. "So you are specialist workers. You need yellow cards."

"Oh," says Mama with a faint smile. I can see she is pleased to be called a "specialist".

Omama is too old to be registered for work. She

throws her hands up at the harassed staff from the Jewish Council and protests, but she is informed that she can stay at home and keep house for us.

Mama is told that we will not receive any pay for our work.

I open my mouth to complain at this but she shoves me in the ribs and turns me round before I have a chance to say anything that we might all regret.

Thank God Omama does not hear the bit about us not receiving pay.

Our registration is finished. We make our way down *Sadovņikova iela* and into *Ludzas iela.*

We brush past other Jews who are stopping and consulting one another, trying to find their lodgings. I try not to look too closely at the buildings we are passing but I can't help it. Many of them are only one storey high and their thin walls are made of cheap wooden slats. Several windows are smashed or missing altogether and there are boards nailed up over the gaps. One or two of the houses have no roofs although others have pointed gables and might have been pretty, about a hundred years ago. There are dogs chained to walls and barking in the run-down front gardens of some of the houses. I guess their owners had to leave them behind if they were moving in to smart apartments in town so that Jews could move into these dilapidated houses.

"I know this area," says Omama. "When I was a girl, I used to visit my friend here. It is a nice place, no?"

We ignore her sarcastic tone.

"Very near the Jewish cemetery, too," says Omama, waving her arm in front of us. "Most handy."

When Omama is in this mood it is best to ignore her. Mama stops, out of breath, and sits for a moment on the side of her barrow. We are outside number 29. It is a fragile building of three storeys. There is an attic window in the roof. The wooden walls are brown and the windows are thick with grey dirt and bordered by sills whose paint has long since rotted away. There are wooden shutters hanging off the ground-floor windows and the roof is missing several slates.

I stare at this place which is to be our new home and realize that the apartment in *Skārņu iela* was really not as bad as we had always thought it. This building is in a different league altogether.

"Well!" says Mama in the bright voice she always assumes when she senses my fear. "We'd better get in and start unpacking."

She steps forward and pushes the main door. It swings open with a creak and a small bird flies out into her face and makes her scream.

We navigate our barrows into a dark hallway. Although it smells of damp and something less pleasant, there are brown panels on the walls which may once have been smart and there are holes where picture hooks were inserted.

Mama is looking around with a frown.

"This was a family home," she says. "It must have been divided into apartments by the Soviets. I hope the previous residents are having better luck than us."

"Well," says Omama, "those penniless Russians will now be put into the apartments we Jews left. Of course they will have better luck than us! For the first time they will have electricity and running water!"

Mama has abandoned her barrow at the foot of the stairs and is climbing up, hanging onto what is left of the banister. The stairs creak and there is a smell of mould and dust and overflowing rubbish.

"This must be ours," she calls from the first floor. "There is nobody else here."

I help Omama up two flights and we enter the apartment which is to be our new home.

There is only really one main room, with a wooden floor with split floorboards and one uncurtained window overlooking the street. Off this room is a tiny kitchen with one sink, a greasy stove and nothing else. There is a small bedroom which opens out of the opposite side of the living room but there is no furniture in it. There is no dining room and no bathroom but Mama finds a toilet in what looks like a cupboard.

"It is not even the space we have been promised," says Mama, her face falling. "They said that each Jew would have three to four square metres of living space. I don't think it is even quite that."

Her face looks so anxious that I smile.

"We are thin," I say. "We don't need so much space anyway."

Omama laughs. She fiddles about in her pocket and produces something in a silver wrapper.

"And we have two squares of chocolate," she says, passing me a piece. "So we will not get much fatter, but we will be happy."

I allow the soft, sweet lump of darkness to dissolve on my tongue.

"Mama!" says my mother. "Where on earth did you get chocolate? We have not been near a proper grocery store for months!"

My grandmother cackles with pleasure. She opens the silver foil and divides up the rest of her spoils.

"I used to be on good terms with my Rabbi," she says. "I saved it for a moment such as this." My mother is shaking her head in despair but she takes her piece of chocolate and sucks on it with a look of bliss on her face. Then she claps her hands as if getting rid of something and says: “Right, girls. We’d better start cleaning up in here.”

We clean for the rest of the day and still we do not manage to get the apartment the way that we would like it.

Mama has brought soap and kerosene in her barrow and it is just as well. No sooner have I started to lay down my pillows and blankets in the corner of the main room than a large mouse scuttles out of a corner and bolts across the floor. Omama has found a nest of cockroaches in the small bedroom where she is going to sleep and when I sit down on the floor to rest my sleep-deprived limbs for a moment I get bitten to death by fleas and have to be rubbed down at the one sink by Mama with her large bar of yellow soap.

I clean the floor of our living room several times with the mop-head that we brought from our old apartment but it takes me three hours to get the dirt and stains off.

By the time the evening comes we are beyond exhausted.

I am sitting on the tiny ledge in front of the window. Mama has fashioned us a curtain out of some of her old material and I am watching Jews arriving in the ghetto while I sniff the nice clean smell of her rose-printed fabric.

Mama puts together the bread and cheese she has brought from home and although the bread is stale and the cheese speckled with a grey-green mould, we are so hungry that we devour it, sitting in a circle on the floor and using a wooden box as a table. Omama sits on a folded-up shawl to stop her bony bottom hurting on the floorboards. I sit cross-legged. The muscles I used to have in my legs from ballet have wasted away. I prod them and watch the dimples which do not disappear.

"I should do my exercises," I say.

"Never mind your legs," says Mama. "I must find out where we get our food." She goes into the tiny kitchen and turns the rusty tap. A stream of grey-looking water comes out. "There will be a place here somewhere."

She passes round the glasses of dirty water and we try to drink.

"Nothing more for me tonight," says Omama. "I have never ached so much in my life. I would sleep on a nest of cockroaches, even if they had giant teeth."

"You do not have to now," says Mama with a tired smile. She is almost asleep where she sits. I am the same. We have not slept since the last night in Uncle Georgs's attic before we were disturbed by the ringing of the grey alarm bell.

Omama goes into her tiny bedroom and curls up on the bed we have made her from blankets, pillows and leftover fabrics.

Mama and I have made a floor-bed each on opposite sides of the living room. My makeshift bed lies underneath a small painting of St Peter's Church that Mama brought from home. It once hung on the wall of my bedroom in our beautiful villa and whenever I see that painting I feel at home. The brown triple-layered spire stretches up towards a bright red sunset and the River Daugava splits the city in two with its dark waters and humped bridge that always reminds me of a serpent in a children's book.

I do not feel very at home in this room, however.

It is strange not having a mattress or any furniture.

Mama says goodnight and goes to sleep straight away.

I lie in my heap of blankets and listen to the street noise outside. Sometimes there is the sound of people crying or arguing and the slamming of doors. I can still hear the rumble of wheels from carts and barrows late into the night as more families arrive to seek their new lodgings.

I lie awake worrying about what will happen to us and wishing I knew what had happened to Papa. All I know is that he was put into a cattle truck and taken away, and I have always tried to picture him with work and food and a roof over his head but it is starting to occur to me that nothing I previously thought is true. After all, I thought Velna was my best friend and that Uldis was my boyfriend and that these two facts would never change.

"Ha," I say to myself in the darkness with a small, sarcastic laugh.

I return to thinking about Papa. He is a good man. That at least will never change. But what if he is also shoved into a ghetto somewhere with not enough food or warm clothes? How would I know? How will I find him again when the war is over, or how will he find me?

I know one thing for certain, though. I promised Papa that I would look after Mama and Omama and so I have to keep my promise, especially after everything that has just happened.

I feel sick with guilt. I have not done a very good job of honouring that promise.

After what feels like hours I stop thinking.

My last thought is: *Maybe it won't be so bad here. I am still with my family.*

I sleep without dreaming until morning.

Chapter Thirteen

We wake to a hammering on the door downstairs.

"*Mein Gott!*" croaks Omama. "Can't they let an old woman sleep?"

That is typical of my grandmother. She is complaining that she is young enough to work and yet now she is saying that she is too old to be woken up in the middle of the night.

It is dark outside. The rain drips down our dirty grey windowpanes.

"Report to work!" comes the cry from a Latvian policeman outside. "All Jews must report to work!"

We struggle into seated positions from our uncomfortable bedding on the floor. Mama stretches her back with a grimace and looks at the wristwatch which she has hidden under her blankets.

"It is five o'clock," she says. "No wonder I feel tired."

I braid my hair as fast as possible. The plaits hang limp and greasy over my shoulders but there is no time to wash and no warm water to wash in, only the thin grey stream of liquid from the kitchen sink tap. I am still wearing my clothes from yesterday so I just leave them on.

Mama and I put our coats with the yellow stars on.

"Wear all your clothes under the coat, Hanna," she says. "It is very cold outside."

The weather in Rīga turns from boiling hot to freezing cold in the space of a few days.

I slip my jacket on and become Hanna the Jew with the yellow stars again.

At least I will not stand out from the crowds that are gathering outside.

There is no time to eat breakfast and in any case we are down to only a small amount of bread.

We have to say goodbye to Omama. It is the first time the three of us have split up during the daytime since she came to live with us in *Skārņu iela* in June.

Her eyes look small and frightened in her wrinkled face but her hands are strong as they push us towards the door.

"Go," she says. "Somebody has to earn a wage around here."

Mama looks as if she is about to speak and then changes her mind.

There are things that it is better Omama does not know.

We scurry over the wet cobbles that line the ghetto streets.

A steady stream of Jews dressed just like us in thick coats and sweaters with their two yellow stars visible are hurrying towards the main ghetto gate. We link arms and follow them, heads bent against the driving rain, as they pass down *Ludzas iela* and into *Sadovņikova iela,* which leads to the main ghetto gate.

On the other side of the barbed-wire fence, a handful of Latvians are walking back and forth and going to work just as they always did. A few early risers walk their dogs, men hurry along in business suits or in caps and long black winter coats. Night workers are coming home from offices and factories, their walk slow and satisfied at the thought of home, food and sleep.

These people glance at us through the fence as if we are curiosities and then they lower their eyes and hurry ahead.

We assemble at the ghetto gate. There are only four Latvian guards on duty to control all these people but they are accompanied by the ever-present snarling dogs.

"Yellow cards this way," says one of the guards. He does not look any of us in the eye.

We shuffle into a column and are marched through the gates and out of the ghetto.

"Keep in line," says Mama in my left ear. "Do as they say. It will not be long until we get to our workplace and can warm up."

My stomach growls with a sick hunger. I hope they will feed us at this place.

We are marched down *Gogoļa iela* and past the jagged remains of the burned-out Great Choral Synagogue. A lump forms in my throat when I see the stones and blackened wood and remember the beautiful rich fabrics and gold furnishings inside.

Our walk takes us straight down the *Brīvības bulvāris*, past the *Opera* and the park and the *Brīvības piemineklis*, our Freedom Monument where I first saw the line of young Jewish men being marched away.

These are the places I have loved all my life but now I see them through a blur of tears.

I am a stranger in my own city.

We walk for over half an hour in the rain and wind.

My face feels numb and raw and my nose drips.

Our destination is *Ganu iela* on the other side of the old town.

There is a large square building in the street and we are marched straight inside and into a crowded foyer.

It is chaos.

Nobody knows why we are here or what we are supposed to be doing.

I cling onto Mama's arm as hard as I can. I feel the now-familiar fear, deep down in the pit of my stomach and moving into my legs.

There are men working their way amongst the crowds, men from the SS with their stiff uniforms and their shoulders and caps emblazoned with eagles' wings.

One of them stops and looks at Mama. Even with her headscarf on and her face thin from lack of proper food, Mama is still beautiful enough to cause people to take a second glance.

"Very nice," he says in a voice betraying no emotion. "You wish to work here?"

Mama nods.

The SS points at Mama's arm. She has put on her wristwatch out of habit.

"Oh, no," I say. The words just burst out of me. "You can't touch that."

The man laughs, as if I've just told a good joke.

"Gold, yes?" he says. "Take it off."

Mama fumbles with the catch. Her hands are trembling. She holds up the little watch to the light and it glints and sparkles. On the back is the inscription from Papa which he had engraved to mark their tenth wedding anniversary. It says "From Niklas to Kristina, with all my love for ever."

The SS man reads the inscription and his smile widens even further.

"Such a romantic message," he says. "So how about I take care of this for you? You want a job here, yes? You will be kept warm and off the streets."

Mama's eyes grow dim as the man slips her watch into his breast pocket.

"We will work," she says. "After all, what else have we left?"

The SS man has moved along the line, bored of us already.

Later we find out that this man is famous for taking bribes from Jews and giving them slave labour and no money in return.

But it means we are indoors all day and might get fed, whereas we see others thrown out onto the streets where they are forced to sweep the gutters and clear the rubble from ruined houses in the rain.

I guess we should be grateful that Papa gave Mama that watch.

We are working at the *Heereskraftpark.* It is an army vehicle park run by the SS but we are in a workshop making uniforms for the German army, the *Wehrmacht.* The workshop is at the back of the building and is crammed with Jewish women just like us, all bent over machines for twelve hours a day.

I have to follow what Mama is doing and I have to learn it fast. Any false move and the guards who patrol the rows of machines inspecting our work will throw me out into the streets.

I watch as she slides the fabric under the needle of the machine and I copy her and try to remember what she taught me. We are working with tough khaki materials and it is a struggle to penetrate the fabric but I focus all my concentration into what I am doing.

I have to tie my plaits back on the top of my head because they dangle too close to the needle. My hands become dry from handling the fabrics and my eyes ache from squinting but I daren't stop.

We work from six in the morning until midday and then we are allowed to take a break. A piece of bread and a small cup of watery soup are dispensed to each of us. It does not taste good but it stops my stomach from trying to eat itself.

Mama and I go and stand out in the back courtyard where some of the workers are huddled together in the rain, drinking the hot soup.

"Eva!" says Mama, going over to a group of women. "Eva Petersohn!"

The two women embrace. Mama has known Eva since the days when we lived in our villa. Her daughter Zilla is also here. I went to Jewish school with Zilla when I was little.

"I did not know you were a seamstress," I say to Zilla. Her face, once round and glowing, has taken on a sallow, sharp edge, but her eyes are dancing as much as they ever did.

"I am not," she whispers. "And neither is Mama. But don't tell anybody."

I laugh.

"Me neither," I say. "I have sewn an arm to a leg. The poor soldier will not be able to put his uniform on at all!"

We laugh under our breath and then stop quickly. Even out here, the SS pace up and down and glare at us.

There is little time to catch up with our acquaintances

before a whistle is blown and we hustle back to our workstations.

In the afternoon we repair uniforms which have come into the workshop full of holes.

Some of the holes are caused by bullets.

I try not to think about what might have happened to the soldiers wearing them.

I follow Mama's example and keep my head down and my hands busy but inside I am screaming the same refrain over and over.

Is this to be my life now?

Will we get through it and somehow get back to normal?

Will I ever find Papa?

Why did I have to be born a Jew?

At six o'clock on the dot we are told to stop work.

"I have taken my lunch bread for Omama," Mama whispers as we wait with the crowd. "It is well hidden, don't worry."

We reform in our column and are marched back across Rīga and towards the ghetto. The rain has become lighter, but a thin layer has frozen and the gutters are hazardous. I am glad that Omama has not had to come with us.

At the ghetto gate a guard calls "Halt!" and we stop,

just avoiding tipping over the back of the person in front of us.

A Latvian policeman walks along our line. He is asking people to turn out their pockets.

A woman near the front empties her pockets. Two pieces of black bread fall onto the road and lie there, dark against the grey.

There is a struggle. The woman falls to the ground and lies motionless.

The crowd screams out in horror.

Lines of red snake out from behind the woman's head.

Mama's face shows her shock for only a moment. When the policeman reaches us she gives him a small smile and a polite nod.

"I have no food," she says. "It would be stupid to risk my life that way, no?"

She sounds as if she has a toothache. Maybe she has. She has wound her scarf tightly around her chin and cheeks.

But the policeman makes her turn out the pockets on her coat and the pockets on her dress and apron underneath.

Nothing.

We reach our apartment at 29 *Ludzas iela* and at last can shake off the guards.

Mama closes the downstairs door against the cold and spits something out of her cheek.

"Not perhaps the nicest thing," she says. "But it is food."

I stare at my mother in horror.

"They could have seen that," I say. "They might have shot you, too."

But Mama is already heading upstairs to our apartment.

Omama is waiting for us in the main room. She kisses Mama and gives me a painful cheek-pinch.

"I would like to say that I have prepared you a beautiful dinner," she says. "But the reality is somewhat different. Nonetheless I have been to the ghetto shop. In fact that is all I have done. The queue lasted nearly the entire day."

She gestures towards the box that we use as a table.

There is a small amount of meat on three plates alongside some mouldy potatoes.

"Meat," says Mama, her eyes widening. "Thank God."

"Do not get too excited," says Omama. "The meat has to last us for a whole week and I would not be surprised if it came from a dog. I only got the potatoes because I bribed the man in the shop."

"Oh yes?" says Mama. "And what did you give to the shopkeeper in exchange?"

Omama busies herself with filling up our cups with dirty tap water.

It is then that I realize.

She is walking without her carved wooden stick. Or limping, to be more exact.

"You didn't?" I say. "But you can't get around without that!"

"Oh, Mama," says my mother, sinking down onto the floor and staring at the potatoes. They are full of black eyes. She picks one up and her finger goes right through into the middle with a soft *phut* noise. "It is not worth it for these! You should not have given him your stick."

"Well, I had to do something," says Omama. "It is too dangerous for non-Jews to come in here now with extra food. Soon the bastard Nazis will lock us all away from the rest of the city for good."

Mama is crying.

I look at her, astonished. All day she has been so strong and brave.

"I don't mind working," she says between sobs. "But I hate that my daughter must work twelve hours a day too and that my mother has given away her walking stick to help feed us. That is wrong. WRONG."

Omama limps over and places her hand on Mama's shoulder.

"We do what we must," she says in a voice so soft and

unlike Omama that it sounds as if another woman has sneaked into our apartment and crept up behind us.

Mama nods, gulps and pats her hair.

"Sorry," she says. "Long day. Anyway, I brought you some bread, Mama."

The three of us stare down at the small soggy black pile of mush that has spent the last couple of hours living inside Mama's cheek.

My cheek begins to twitch. I daren't look at Omama.

She lets out a great splutter of amusement.

"I will go and get three spoons," she says. "We will not waste this treat."

And with that, our family limps back to life for another night.

Chapter Fourteen

THERE ARE SIXTEEN SHOPS FOR JEWS inside our ghetto.

By the end of the first week we are familiar with all of them.

Mama sends me out at the weekend to queue alongside the rest of the ghetto residents.

The food is brought in by Jewish wagoners who have been allowed out into the city to collect it.

There are strict rations for Jews. We are allowed one hundred and seventy-five grams of meat, one hundred grams of butter and two hundred grams of sugar a week. For those who have extra money there are still non-Jews who take the risk to smuggle in dried food and smoked and canned goods and charge three times the usual price for them.

Mama manages to get three cans of smoked fish by selling a piece of her jewellery, a pendant necklace of gold and amber.

A lot of people are burying their valuables by night.

I watch them from the window seat upstairs at number 29. They creep out during the night under cover of darkness. They dig deep slanted holes near trees and then bury their goods wrapped in sacks inside sealed cans. Then they cover over the holes until there is no trace.

Sometimes I wonder if in fifty years' time, somebody will buy these houses and dig up their gardens to plant carrots and potatoes and instead find a family's hidden gold and silver underneath.

We have a few trinkets left to sell and a little money which Mama has managed to put by. It is left over from when she was a busy seamstress in the old town.

We use this money to queue up and buy our meagre rations once a week.

The rest of the time we spend at work.

Mama has developed a cough.

She is running a fever on Wednesday morning when the work columns are due to assemble. Omama tells her to stay at home and rest but Mama has heard rumours of what happens if the SS raid your apartment and find you not at work so she struggles into her coat and boots and wraps her scarf right round her mouth to try and stifle the cough.

My heart contracts at the sight of Mama's shoulders shaking as she tries to lessen the noise.

The SS do not like illness and disease. Mama says that they are frightened of an epidemic breaking out in the ghetto that they might catch. At the same time the ghetto has no method of disposing of garbage and sewage and the streets are starting to smell bad so the Jewish Council begin to dig large pits and bury rubbish inside them and they arrange for the sewage to be collected and buried in other pits nearby.

It is the 1st October and Yom Kippur today. This is the most important date on the Jewish calendar. In our old life that would mean that we had a day of fasting followed by an evening at the synagogue with dramatic chantings and beatings of our hearts with our right hands. It is a day of atonement where we are supposed to remember our deceased relatives and make up with those we have quarrelled with.

This Yom Kippur is somewhat different. It goes like this:

Mama and I struggle to work. Instead of fasting we are

desperate for the bread and soup which is passed around the workers at midday.

At six o'clock we stop work and are marched in columns across the town towards the ghetto.

We find Omama trying to observe the day of fasting but Mama puts her foot down and forces Omama to eat a small piece of meat and half a rotten potato and a strange sort of sweet bread that Mama has managed to make out of our sugar ration and a tiny amount of flour that she had to pay over the odds for.

Mama's cough is so much worse that Omama asks me to go and visit the clinic on *Katoļu iela* and get her some medicine. This clinic has been set up by the Jewish Council for ghetto residents. I go in through the main doors feeling sick with nerves and I have to wait for over an hour to be seen, but in fact the Jewish doctors and their one nurse, Bobé, are kind and efficient. They give me some syrup for Mama's cough and say that I must bring her in if it gets worse.

I walk back to *Ludzas iela* clutching my medicine bottle with pride. It feels good to have done something useful for Mama.

I have been out for a total of about ninety minutes.

You would not think that anything could change so much in that time.

That is what I used to think before I lived in the ghetto.

As I climb up the stairs to our apartment I hear raised voices.

Amidst the clamour I can hear poor Mama trying to make herself heard and then dissolving into bursts of coughing. I can also hear Omama using her sharpest and most sneering tone of voice, which is never a good sign.

I walk into the main room with my medicine bottle clutched close to my chest and I stop dead.

There are three extra people in our apartment.

Five faces turn towards me as I walk in.

For a moment I am so confused that I can't even pick out the faces of Mama and Omama.

For a moment I think I am in the wrong apartment.

But no. My mother and grandmother are standing in one corner of the room and opposite them by the wall stands a family of strangers.

There is a boy of about my age with a sharp, narrow face and a sweep of dark hair. He is holding the hand of a little girl with the same dark hair tied up with a pink ribbon. Next to them stands a man about Mama's age with greying hair. He is wearing a brown leather cap, a brown jacket and has dirty brown work boots on his feet.

All three of them are thin and angular, like they're made of coat-hanger wire. I'm starting to see that look a lot around here. I can see it on my own face when I dare to look in the dirty mirror on the wall in the tiny toilet.

"Hanna," says Mama, trying not to cough. "Did you get the medicine?"

I nod and slip her the bottle. The little girl looks at the bottle as if she would like to have some of the contents.

Sugar, I think. It is cough syrup. We could probably live for a week on this bottle alone.

Omama goes to get a spoon.

I stare at the three strangers. They stare back at me. They all have the same worried brown eyes and thick dark brows.

"Is anybody going to tell me what's going on?" I say. Once upon a time I would have been more polite and waited for Mama to introduce them. The ghetto seems to be knocking all traces of manners and decorum out of me.

"I'll tell you," says Omama, pouring Mama's medicine onto a spoon and gesturing for Mama to open her mouth and swallow. "We have new room-mates, that's what. These people want to live with us."

Horror rises up from my feet and threatens to throttle me.

I go into the tiny kitchen and start throwing together our evening "meal", such as it is. There is no point even trying to fast. We are too weak and need all the food we can get. I swallow and try not to think what we would have eaten on the day before Yom Kippur in our old life. Saliva moistens my tongue as I picture the home-made chicken soup, golden and savoury and studded with fragrant, soft matzo balls that would have lined our stomachs for the day of fasting ahead.

Tonight we have what is called the "ghetto speciality" around here. Zilla and her mother told us how to make it. It is basically a liver paste made from yeast. Yeast is cheap so we can get a lot of it. At first I thought it was disgusting but it's amazing what you can get used to when you are hungry. I have fried up the potato peelings from last night on the tiny stove and I spread the liver paste on top of them. We have more of the weird sugar-and-flour cake that Mama made earlier in the week so I put that out as well, along with the black bread which Mama still smuggles in from the workshop on *Ganu iela* when she can.

The three strangers are standing where I left them.

I put the food on the box and raise my eyebrows at Mama and Omama.

My look is supposed to say, "Okay, game up. Get rid of the visitors now. Time to eat."

Omama frowns at me.

"Ach, I can't go on fighting," she says. "I am too old for battle inside the house as well as out. Yom Kippur is a day of making up with people," she says. "We are all human beings in this room tonight."

Mama sips red liquid from the spoon and doesn't speak. She is looking at me, trying to gauge my reaction.

Then she looks over at our uninvited visitors. I follow her gaze. Three pairs of dark brown eyes have swivelled their focus onto the food that we have put on our box-table. The little girl's eyes are wide with longing. Her legs are like lollipop sticks in stout lace-up boots and grubby white socks. The boy has a thick black woollen jacket but there are holes in the knees of his trousers. The man has kind eyes underneath the yearning expression.

I sigh and go back into the kitchen. I feel very old and wise and tired.

I get the rest of the week's "ghetto speciality" and put it out on the box.

"Okay," I say. "Dinner is served."

The little girl stares up at me with a mouth already smeared with paste.

I feel like I'm their guardian angel.

*

Over the scraps of food we talk.

Mama coughs, but Omama and I ask questions.

The man's name is Janis and he was born here just like me. His children are called Max and Sascha. Max is sixteen and Sascha only four.

"Where is your wife?" I ask. Mama does an extra-loud cough on purpose to stop me asking such personal questions but I figure if these people are sitting here wolfing down my peelings-and-yeast speciality then I have a right to know a bit about them.

Janis continues to stuff food into his mouth and lick his fingers but his eyes take on a wary look. He has not removed his leather cap or his coat. It is colder inside this apartment than it is outside in the ghetto streets.

"You remember the first days of the Nazi invasion?" he says. "When there was fighting and a lot of apartments were looted and Jews killed?"

The three of us nod. It is hard to forget the screams and sounds of gunshots and burning buildings.

"My wife, Sara, was shot," he says, in a matter-of-fact voice. He reaches out for more peelings and puts them in front of Sascha. "She died in my arms. The children were watching."

I stop eating. I am hungry but somehow I can't pick up another morsel.

"Hanna," says Mama. "Go and make some coffee for our guests."

Omama has managed somehow to buy a tiny amount of ersatz coffee from the Jewish shops in the ghetto. The coffee tastes nothing like coffee used to before the war but it is hot and black and something to offer the others, so I go in and boil up water in a small grey rusty saucepan and pour it into the assorted cups that we brought in our barrow from *Skārņu iela.*

I cut pieces of Mama's strange sugar-cake and divide it up amongst the five of us. It amounts only to an inch cubed each but Sascha eats it as if it is the very best chocolate torte in the whole of Rīga. I look at Max. He has kept his head down so far, concentrating on the food. I notice that his fingernails are very dirty.

"Do you work?" I ask him, but it is his father who answers.

"Well of course," he says. "We have to work. What choice is there?"

I flush. It was a bit of a stupid question.

"Where?" I say.

"Army warehouse," says Janis. "We sort coats and boots captured from the Soviets."

That explains his solid work boots and Max's thick, warm black coat. I am envious of that coat. Mine is thin and patchy and the yellow stars are starting to flap at their seams.

"Where have you been sleeping?" I ask. I can't seem to stop my voice sounding harsh and suspicious. The truth is, I don't want these people living with us and sharing our food. I have got used to it just being the three of us.

"On the floor of a house in *Līksnas iela*," says Janis. "Before that, on the streets. We were one of the last families to enter the ghetto. There was no room left."

I am about to pop my square of cake into my mouth but a beseeching look from the little girl stops me with my hand halfway to my lips.

"Oh, go on then," I say, passing it to her. "I'm too tired to eat anyway."

That part at least is true. I ache from a day hunched over a sewing machine under the cold eyes of the SS and from the long walk to and from the workshop.

"What happens to Sascha when you go to work?" I say, yawning. It is nearly ten o'clock and we must be up at five for work again the next day.

Janis pulls the little girl onto his lap.

"She is looked after by whichever kind lady happens to offer," he says. Then he gives a sly look at Omama.

"Oh no," she says. "I am not a nursery. I am an old woman without a stick. I cannot chase after a little child all day."

Janis's face falls. He looks at me and then at Mama.

"Sorry," she says. "We work all day every day."

Omama puts her hands together as in prayer and rolls her eyes.

"God help me," she says. "It is Yom Kippur. He knows full well that I can't disobey His wishes on such a holy day."

Then my grandmother, with a great creaking of knee joints and much moaning and sucking of teeth, levers herself towards the floor. She peers into Sascha's doubtful little face and then offers the greatest compliment that she knows – an Omama cheek-pinch.

The child's face crumples to scarlet and she howls in fear and pain.

Omama's face lights up like the inside of the *Doma laukums* in our beloved old town.

"I can see we're going to get along just fine," she announces.

And that is how we come to share our apartment with three complete strangers.

*

We establish a routine of sorts.

We have to, or we would all trip over one another and tempers would fray. Mama sits up late one night and composes our rotas. There is a rota for who uses the toilet and the kitchen sink first in the morning. There is a rota for who makes the supper and who puts together the meagre breakfast. There is a rota for who goes out to queue for weekly rations.

The sleeping arrangements are as follows:

Mama, Omama, Sascha and I now sleep in the main room together. We call it "The Girls' Room". When the four of us are lying in our makeshift beds on the wooden floorboards, there seems very little air or space left in the room.

Max sleeps in the tiny box room where Omama used to sleep. There is only enough room for one person there so Janis sleeps on the floor of the kitchen, rolled up in a blanket and with his jacket folded up for a pillow.

It is hard to get to sleep, what with Omama muttering and cursing in her sleep, Mama coughing, Janis snoring and Sascha crying or being sick.

The only one who makes no noise is Max. I have yet to work him out. We haven't exchanged one word since he moved in.

There is also an unwritten agreement that our new

tenants must contribute to the food pot in any way that they can. Janis and Max have got a non-Jewish friend on the outside of the ghetto who passes in the opposite direction to their work column and slips them food at a particular point on their march to the army warehouse once every three days. In this way we get carrots, onions and more rotten potatoes, anything small and round which can be concealed in an inside pocket or a hand, but it helps to supplement our tiny rations from the ghetto grocer's shops.

Janis and Max also get black bread and sometimes cheese or a piece of hard sausage at the place where they work and they eat some and risk smuggling the rest. This is very dangerous as the guards still search people on arrival back at the ghetto gates, but starving people take risks.

We all do. Mama still hides black bread in her mouth, between her breasts and once even somewhere far more horrible.

Her face was full of shame and self-disgust.

It is what we have to do to survive.

Sascha is too little to smuggle food but even she knows how to rummage through the piles of garbage that mount up behind the ghetto houses and once she came in triumphant with half a loaf of mouldy bread and something which at first looked like a pile of droppings, but turned out to be some ancient peas.

We share our hoard at the end of every day. If we hear the SS bursting into the houses nearby for one of their random Jew-checks, we throw all the food and dishes into the lavatory and shut the lid. The SS do not like to touch anything which may be riddled with germs or disease. When the risk has passed we get it all out again and wipe off the worst of the damage before eating the meal as planned.

Just a few weeks ago the thought of doing this would have seemed disgusting.

But I am no longer the Hanna Michelson who lived in the beautiful villa in Rīga or even the temporary apartment on *Skārņu iela.* The Hanna who loved Uldis and believed that he loved her back. The Hanna with a pretty best friend named Velna and a kind Uncle Georgs. The Hanna who dreamed of becoming a famous ballet dancer on the stage of the Rīga *Opera*.

How did I lose so much in so little time?

I am not the same Hanna any more.

The barbed wire fences and gates around the ghetto are nailed into position on 25th October.

On the way back from work Mama reads out the sign at the ghetto gates.

Those who try to climb across the fence or try to communicate with the ghetto internees will be shot down without warning.

"We are like animals trapped in a zoo," I say.

We are back in our apartment. From here we can't quite see the main ghetto gate but we can see the command post at the end of our street. We are watching the guards who pace up and down here. Some of them are SS, some Latvian and now we have our own Jewish Ghetto Police who are there to keep order. They wear caps and uniforms with a blue Star of David on them.

"Worse," says Omama. She ignores Mama's sharp look. I guess Omama knows that I have had to grow up pretty fast over the last year. It is impossible to hide the truth from me any longer. "Animals in a zoo would be fed twice a day with fresh meat. And they would not be shot."

As night falls the temperature drops.

"Winter is starting early this year," says Mama. She plugs up the gaps around our windows with bits of fabric from her sewing basket but still our breath freezes on the air inside the main room. "I don't remember it starting at the end of October in quite this way before."

Tonight feels different. This time last week we could still have got out of the ghetto if we had wanted to risk our lives and try to hide back in the old town. Visitors were still finding their way in with food and aid. Non-Jewish friends and relatives visited the old people's home or the hospital.

Now we are sealed off in this island crammed to the limits with homeless Jews.

There are thirty thousand of us in the ghetto. All crammed into sixteen blocks.

It feels different, the night they seal the ghetto.

I feel different too. All the lasts bits of my innocence have been stripped away, never to return. And I feel more determined, which is odd because I am also suffering a rising rush of fear and anxiety about how we will survive in here on our cut-off island.

I promised Papa that I would look after my family. And I promised myself that whatever happens I will try to get out of here alive so that I can find Papa.

There are some things I can't control, though.

I wake in the middle of the night with my teeth chattering. Over the noise of Janis snoring from the kitchen and Mama coughing in her sleep, I hear muffled noise from the street outside, as if it is coming from Omama's forbidden radio buried underneath a pile of blankets.

I ease myself up from the floor, stiff with the cold. There are freezing draughts of air coming in through the gaps in the window frame so I wrap myself in a blanket and pull aside Mama's curtains.

Outside, an SS vehicle is making its way down *Ludzas iela*. The muffled noise was its tyres crunching along a mass of white.

A mass of swirling flakes takes my breath away.

The twenty-fifth of October.

The day they seal the ghetto.

The day the first snow comes.

Chapter Fifteen

WE ESTABLISH OUR ROUTINE AND we stick to it for nearly four weeks.

I can't remember living any other way.

My life is now that of an adult worker. I get up at five, wash with dirty water, gulp a cup full of weak black coffee and eat any small hard piece of bread that we might have managed to put by.

Janis has to get up, visit the toilet and then return to the kitchen so that Mama and I, as the female workers, can get ourselves ready in what little privacy we have left. He sits by the sink, his eyes red-rimmed from cold, and feeds Sascha with whatever he can find.

Max comes in from his box room, white from lack of sleep and with dark shadows around his eyes. He is sixteen but some mornings looks sixty.

I expect I look this way too.

I try to avoid looking in the dirty mirror if I can help it. I know that my plump olive-skinned cheeks are sallow and sharp and that my hair is lank and greasy from no proper shampoo.

I lie in bed at night trying to recall if I was pretty or not. Sometimes I think of Uldis and my heart misses a beat. I can't forgive his betrayal and the way in which he manipulated me into telling him where we were hiding, but a persistent little voice in my head reminds me that it was I who told him where to find us. And somewhere buried even deeper underneath the guilt is still a tiny shred of belief that Uldis can't truly be all bad. I torture myself with images of the friendship we used to have before the war even started. He smiles down at me in broad sunlight. He teases me with that slow, lazy look in his eye. That insolent grin.

Then I see the crumpled bodies of my aunt and uncle and sometimes I stuff a handkerchief in my mouth so as to muffle the sound of my crying and silently I pray that they might forgive me for my actions.

I am starting to loathe Uldis Lapa.

How could such a good friend turn so rotten right down to his very core?

Although I feel sick when I think about him, I still feel compelled to look out for Uldis when I march to and from my workplace. I never see him.

It's probably a good thing. I am not sure I could control my anger. And he probably wouldn't recognize the new, dirty, skinny and ungroomed Hanna who looks like she needs a good scrub with soap and water.

We all do. There is only that one rusty sink and the water comes out brown or grey but never clear like you'd want it to. Mama rations out the bars of soap she brought from home. The sharp clean pine smell makes tears of homesickness rush up to my eyes.

As well as feeling dirty, I am constantly hungry. My stomach produces sick, sour acid which rushes up into my mouth and my guts rumble all the time. I have started to take stupid risks, trading with non-Jewish visitors to the *Heereskraftpark* during my lunch break. Everybody does it, but depending on which member of the SS is patrolling the workshops you can get fined, beaten, robbed of lunch, or even shot. Some of the officers from the *Wehrmacht* are more understanding and do not mind if we slip a piece of lunch bread in our pockets.

I have traded in the last small bits of Mama and Omama's jewellery although I felt wracked with sadness at handing over the precious pieces into the hands of strangers.

Mama hid much of it in her clothing when we moved from Uncle Georgs's and we have not buried any of it, despite the constant risk of the SS bursting into our apartment and robbing us.

"What is the point of burying our things?" Mama says. "It is no good to us buried and we may never come back here once the war is over."

She is right. So one day I decide to trade some of my jewellery too.

I sneak a bit of Mama's old lipstick to work and then I say that I have to use the toilet just before lunch.

I slash the red across my mouth and pinch my cheeks to give them a bit of colour.

In my pocket I have a silver and amber necklace that Mama bought me for my thirteenth birthday. I wore it every day until Mama told me that it was dangerous to flash jewellery in the streets after the Nazis invaded.

I am thin now. Thin enough to push myself out of the window at the back of the lavatory and into the courtyard behind where trucks arrive with more uniforms for us to mend.

I wait until one of the men slides out of the high cab of his truck. I cast a quick look back at the factory to check I'm not being watched and I sidle up to him and stand by the side of the truck and the open door in such a way that I can't be seen from the factory.

"What are you doing out here?" says the man. I stand my ground. I have been watching this particular soldier for days now and I reckon he has a kind face. He's a member of the German army but not one of the SS so I have decided that I will take the risk even though my heart is beating fast with the daring of it all.

"I have this," I say, pulling out my pendant and letting it dangle in front of his eyes. The amber catches the light. It is a good piece of Rīga's finest.

The soldier groans but quick as a flash he snatches the necklace and opens a flap at the back of his truck before shoving me inside. For one moment I think he is going to report me and my head pounds with panic but then he follows me in and starts to feel around in some of the knapsacks strewn about inside.

"Here," he says. "This is all I've got. Now get back inside. I should report you."

I flash the man my best smile and hold my hands out.

"Thank you," I say.

Then I shove my bounty into my overall pockets, climb back through the tiny lavatory window, unbolt the door of my cubicle and go back inside the factory as if nothing has happened. The whole transaction has taken less than five minutes.

We get searched when we arrive back at the ghetto and coat pockets are the first place that the guards look so I have got good at hiding things wedged under my chin and wrapped around with a thick scarf or sometimes shoved down my socks. I watch to see who is searched in front of me and I try to get right behind them as soon as I can, because I've realized that the guards check every four or five people along.

And that is how, that evening, I come to bring a meat sandwich, an apple, a half-packet of cigarettes and two bars of chocolate to my delighted family.

Max has managed to get a small amount of canned fish from his contacts on the outside of the ghetto. We share out slivers of pilchard and herring with reverence. This is now the equivalent of a major feast.

We are all risking our lives, but I have decided to carry on risking mine if it means I can feed Mama and Omama. I am starting to see the veins in Mama's neck bulging out and Omama's legs are more like brown shiny twigs than ever. It is filling me with panic. I can't lose Mama or Omama.

I don't have enough spare energy to worry about our room-mates. They can look after themselves.

So every morning Mama and I join the work column marching to *Ganu iela* and Max and Janis join another column to work at the Lenta Factory which is on *Jelgavas iela* so they don't have to walk as far as us. I am envious of that. By the time I have sat for twelve hours in a sewing workshop breathing in the air full of bits of fluff and fabric and staring at the rough khaki material as I push it under the needle, my back and eyes ache with exhaustion, and the long trudge back to the ghetto in the numbing snow of Rīga is tough on my body.

We are all beginning to starve.

Some people in the ghetto are dying of malnutrition and disease. On the way to work we see bodies laid outside apartments in the snow, waiting to be taken to the Jewish Cemetery. Many elderly people have been put in a temporary old people's home near to our apartment. Omama goes there to visit one of her cronies and comes back in a foul mood, wiping away tears.

"They are living in piss and shit," she says. "The place stinks. There is one big room with beds down each side and there are no windows. Nobody is going to get me into that home. I would rather die first."

She glares at me for a moment, making sure that I get the message.

"I will not put you in a home," I say. "Mama might, though," I can't resist adding.

"Rude girl," says Omama, bestowing one of her cheek-pinches on my thin face. It hurts like hell but it's a little taste of home and the tears that it brings are not just from the pain.

Sascha backs away into a corner.

She and Omama have a testy sort of relationship. When the two of them are left alone together in the house, it tries both their patience to the limit. I would never have paired the big-eyed, pretty, four-year-old Sascha with my old, bony, hunched-over grandmother, but that's just the way it has to be in here.

Max and I have started talking a bit now. It's awkward, because we haven't chosen to get to know one another, we've just been thrown together by circumstance.

He's not the sort of boy I would normally like anyway. He's very dark and serious with olive skin and quite the opposite of Uldis with his blond, tanned look.

At first I thought he was rude but then he passed me a bit of the treasured canned fish hoard with a small smile and I thought:

Oh. He's just shy.

After that we had a conversation. I told him about my ambitions to be a ballet dancer at the *Opera* and he told me that he would like to be a lawyer. He doesn't mention his mother and I guess that it's too painful so I hold back from asking even though I want to. Instead, I tell him a little about Papa.

That's different. Papa isn't dead.

I describe my papa's brown arms and long, sensitive hands. I talk about his soft moustache and the sparkle in his brown eyes and the way it felt when he picked me up and how the cherry blossom trees at the bottom of our garden would blur into a solid sheet of white as he spun me round and round while I screamed in mock fear.

I wish I knew that wherever he is, Papa was having a better time of it than the ghetto inmates here.

I tell myself that he is fine, every single day. I have to believe that.

But as each day melts into the next and I watch the other Jewish residents of the ghetto struggle to find food, tiny shreds of hope start to detach from my solid belief and float away on the freezing air.

So we have our routines and we try to stick to them and somehow come together at the end of each day and still keep the Sabbath, if it is a Friday, even though we have no wine or candles or matzo now.

"Prayer is free," says Omama. "We can have as much of that as we want. The Nazis can't take that away from us."

So we pray to our God. As everything else is stripped away it seems more important than ever to rely upon Him.

We ask that He might keep us all alive and perhaps find His way to providing us with a bit more food and I feel that as long as we gather together on a Friday night and say the prayers that somehow we will be all right.

A voice inside me tells me that I am being stupid. A stupid girl who thought that people like Uldis meant what they said and kept their promises.

A girl with a blind faith in a God she can't even see or hear.

I am pitting God against the Nazis and expecting God to win.

Doesn't He always win in the end?

Chapter Sixteen

A SIGN IS PINNED TO the gates of the ghetto on 27th November.

It is Mama who sees it as we trudge back through the snow and ice from our workshop on the other side of town.

"No, no," she says, her voice rising up in panic. Then she lowers her head. Anybody causing a noise in the work columns is likely to be beaten by the Latvian soldiers guarding us. Sometimes just a word out of place can result in a shooting.

When we arrive back at number 29 Mama moves up the stairs like a wiry deer trying to escape the rest of a trampling herd. I have not seen her move so fast in a long while.

I find her with Omama. They are holding hands.

"What does that mean?" Omama is saying. "'Resettled'. It sounds as if we are all moving to another part of the country."

Max and Janis are back from work and putting together our meagre evening meal but at the sound of Omama's raised voice they come out of the tiny kitchen and stare at her with concern. Sascha plays on the wooden floorboards, oblivious to what we are saying.

"Maybe they are taking us to Germany," says Janis. "There are camps there where we could work."

Mama is shaking her head in distress. I notice how thin her neck is, so thin that all the veins seem to bulge outwards.

"It said that we should take up to twenty kilograms of food and clothing," she says. "And there's more. It also said that all able-bodied men between eighteen and sixty should report to *Sadovņikova iela* on the 29th and that they will be put in another area of the ghetto and sent to work in the city!"

Janis goes grey in the face.

He looks at Sascha playing with her ragged doll on the floor and at Max, who is laying out bread on the box.

"We are to be split up?" he says. "No. I won't have it. I will not go."

Omama pats his shoulder.

"You should go," she says. "Who knows where we are all being sent to? At least you will get a place of work and be able to stay warm, maybe get some food. Perhaps you will follow us to wherever we are going."

Janis does not look appeased by Omama's reassurances.

"My children have lost their mother," he says. "And now they will lose their father."

Tears roll down his thin cheeks. Max looks at him, awkward. They exchange expressions of pain and desperation that make the pit of my stomach feel strange.

Mama sits down on the floor and stares at the grey lumps of bread that make up our dinner.

"I wish I could feed you all properly," she says.

There doesn't seem to be anything we can say to this so we sit down and eat the bread in silence.

At the end of the meal Omama produces an extra cigarette for Janis and for once she doesn't tell him off for smoking the room out.

"We will do our best to look after Sascha and Max," she says. "Don't worry."

But the six of us go to bed with worry heavy in our hearts.

Nobody sleeps a wink.

*

The next night is the last Sabbath we will all spend together.

The Gestapo have issued an order to evict people from the apartments around *Kalna, Līksnas* and *Lauvas ielas* and the bottom half of our own street, *Ludzas*, from the 28th November. All we have heard all evening are the sounds of gunshots and screams as the Jewish Police carry out the Gestapo's commands and the Latvian police enforce them.

Max has risked going outside to see whether the work details are still in place. Mama, Omama and I have not dared to leave the apartment. The ghetto is in chaos and nobody seems to know what is going to happen, but Max finds out that the newly-emptied apartments are to be fenced in and made into something called the Small Ghetto.

He is right. We are up in our apartment peering out and can see new fences being nailed hastily into place by Jewish men taken out of the Central Prison for this purpose.

"Look," says Max. "SS Krause."

SS Krause is the ghetto commandant. He is inspecting the streets with other SS men that we haven't seen before. Something in the way that they are walking and conferring, their heads bent together, sends a deep chill into my heart.

"Don't watch, Hanna," says Mama but I can't seem to stop. I am balanced not only on the narrow window sill but on the brink of a whole new life somewhere else. There is danger and unsettledness hanging in the air tonight, mixed up with the unspoken sadness of Janis having to leave us tomorrow morning.

We are unable to sleep again. Mama sits up sewing bags for our possessions and packing everything she thinks we need for our journey into the unknown. She packs what is left of our food supplies into one bag, and as many cups, blankets and pieces of clothing as she can into another.

It is the Sabbath so we sit around our box-table and offer up prayers to God but it is difficult to focus on a God you cannot see when the sounds and smells of danger and fear are all around.

Janis sits up all night with Max squashed close beside him and a sleeping Sascha in his arms. When dawn breaks Mama makes us all a cup of black coffee and distributes what is left of our bread.

The sound of men's feet trudging past comes up to our first-floor window. I glance outside, my eyes stiff from lack of sleep.

"The men are going," I say.

We all turn and look at Janis.

He puts his brown cap on and wraps his coat around his thin frame.

Then he kisses Max on the cheek and Sascha on top of the head.

He does not say a word.

We listen to the clomp of his leather work boots as he goes downstairs.

A moment later we see him join the line of men heading to *Sadovņikova iela.*

Max and Sascha manage not to cry.

I think they must have used up all their tears over the past year.

Instead Mama keeps them busy with packing and tidying and from time to time she catches my eye and I can see how frightened she is, but we do not discuss where we might be going.

She gets me to put on as much underwear as I can manage. She does the same to Sascha. We are very restricted by the twenty kilogram limits.

"Get rid of that bloody thing," she says to Omama. My grandmother is trying to pack her contraband radio into a pile of blankets. "You'll have us all killed."

Omama pulls a face but with reluctance she takes the

small black radio out again and puts it in the kitchen cupboard.

We finish the packing and tidy up all the things we have left behind. Mama cleans the kitchen even though she will not be using it again. It is just something to do with her hands to stop the nerves.

I return to the window like a magnet. I can't keep away. I don't want to see what is happening but another part of me needs to.

The column of men including Janis is forced to stand at the corner of our street for six hours in the cold and snow. I strain to see if I can see him but all the men are wearing brown caps and it is impossible to distinguish one from the other. At the head of the line stand two distinguished members of our Jewish Council. Dr Michail Eljaschew, chairman of the *Judenrat*, wears his black fur coat with the blue and white ribbon identifying him as our council member. Next to him is the Chief Rabbi Mendel Zak with his long grey beard and long dark coat.

At one o'clock on the dot the men are barked at to start moving and they disappear from view.

Max has been watching with me. I see him swallow hard, because his Adam's apple moves up and down, but he says nothing.

There is nothing to say. I can't offer him words of hope because I don't really know if there is any hope to offer.

We wait.

And we wait some more. It gets colder. I huddle in my coat on the window sill, peering through the chink in the curtains.

Mama passes me a cup of hot water because we have no coffee left.

I sip it and watch the steam make patterns on the dirty glass of the window.

We are all very tired from not sleeping the night before but nobody dares to go to sleep now.

Mama paces up and down the main room, chewing her fingers and arguing with Omama over trivial things which don't really matter. They snap and bicker for hours.

Max sits with Sascha on the floor and tries to make up games to divert her from the bickering.

I sit on the window sill and watch the streets.

At seven o'clock columns of armed Latvian police march into the ghetto.

Some of them can hardly walk straight.

"*Mein Gott*," says Omama, following my gaze. "The bastards are drunk."

It begins to get dark.

Shots start to ring out from around the ghetto.

I feel a sour rush of acid come up from my stomach into my mouth.

There is the sound of pounding footsteps in the hallway and several Latvian police burst into our apartment.

For one crazy moment I think that one of them is Uldis and that he has come to save us. The man has similar fair hair and high cheekbones.

But it is not Uldis.

They grab hold of Omama and lift her up.

Mama screams and tries to get hold of Omama's arms.

"You should not be in here, old woman," says one of the men, pushing Mama aside like a piece of rubbish. "There is a home for people like you."

Mama drops to her knees and clasps her hands together, staring up at the man.

"No, she lives with us! Please don't hurt her! My mother is elderly and unwell!"

But it is no good. The police drag Omama out of the door and down the stairs before we can think what to do. Another policeman stops Mama from following by pushing his gun across the doorway.

Max holds Sascha close to him. She is shaking and whimpering with fear.

I am trembling from the top of my greasy scalp right down to my broken leather shoes. I can't believe what just happened.

"Out! Out this minute!" shouts the policeman when he is sure that Omama is gone. "Line up five abreast outside!"

We put our knapsacks on as Mama has told us to.

Then we run downstairs.

Outside on the street there is chaos. The whole of *Ludzas iela* is thronging with people. Some are screaming, others are sobbing quietly. The Latvian police are whipping and shoving people into line.

There is a frost this evening, a crackling frost that bites at our noses and faces.

We stand in lines which are five people wide and we press up against the shoulders of our Jewish brothers and sisters just to keep warm.

Mama is sobbing. She keeps twisting her head right round, her eyes sweeping the streets for signs of Omama.

I am numb with shock.

The wind makes our eyes water and our skin hurt but we stand there for nearly two hours without speaking.

The police disappear.

"Quick," says Mama. "Go back to the house."

I stare at her in astonishment but I know not to argue. I am so cold that the idea of going back to number 29 sounds like Heaven.

We steal back to our apartment building and go upstairs. Other people, strangers, follow us in because our house is close by. We stand about upstairs in our coats, expecting to be ordered outside again but hour after hour passes and nobody comes.

Some people start to sleep standing up, packed together like a box of dominoes.

I am leaning against the wall with Mama's arm around my waist. Max is sitting by the window still holding Sascha.

At some point I must have fallen asleep because I am woken by the shout of a drunken Latvian voice.

"Everybody out! Out!"

The people in our room shake themselves awake and look at one another, eyes blurred by a short sleep. It is seven o'clock the next morning and still dark outside. We go back outside in complete confusion and are told by another policeman that the people on *Ludzas iela* will not be leaving to be resettled today and that we can go back inside to await further instruction.

"These damned Nazis," says Mama as we go back again to our apartment. "They can't even get our evacuation right!"

She sounds just like Omama.

I can't imagine our lives without Omama.

I already miss my grandmother so much that it hurts.

We get no sleep.

As soon as we have put our heavy bags down and heated up some water to drink with our hard bread, a commotion starts outside again.

It is getting light so I can see the long, winding column of people being marched by outside. There are women the same age as Mama and some older ones like Omama. There are children, little girls even younger than Sascha and there are young boys, too, all gripping their mothers' hands.

"Where are they going?" I say. By now we are all peering down at the column of people, desperately trying to see if Omama is amongst them. It grows ever longer and is heading back towards *Maskavas iela,* which leads out of the ghetto.

Mama is about to reply but there is a flurry of gunshots and instead she raises her hands to her mouth in horror.

An SS man has a machine gun. He is firing point-blank into the crowd.

Bodies begin to drop out of the column and crumple into the snow. People trample the dead in their panic to get away from the gunshots. Some of them throw down their bags of precious belongings in order to run faster.

They are whipped by the Latvian police who keep shouting at them to go "Faster! Faster!" They brandish the whips over their heads.

And still the column of people grows and grows.

There are trucks pulled up outside and some of the elderly people are thrown into them. They are piled up on top of one another and then driven off in the same direction as the marching column.

"Hanna," hisses Mama. "Get away from the window unless you want them to shoot you too."

But I cannot move.

Something inside me is whispering that I am watching a dreadful event unfold and that I must remember it. Some part of me has detached from what I am seeing. It's the only way I can keep on watching.

Papa's face flashes into my mind. He is smiling his kindest smile and he has his white shirtsleeves rolled up to show his strong brown wrists and long-fingered hands.

"I wish Papa was here," I whisper through a thick haze of tears.

Mama wraps her arms around my shoulders and pulls me away.

The march goes on until midday.

Then the streets outside fall silent.

There are bodies strewn everywhere. The elderly, the handicapped, the sick and the very young, all murdered for not being able to keep up the pace of the march.

Mama and I sit huddled together, crying. We do not speak much. It is hard to find words to talk about what we have just seen.

When Mama does speak, it is in a whisper.

"Perhaps Omama has been resettled in a better camp," she says. "That is what the rumour was. She will be there now and we will join her soon."

I nod, even though I do not know what to think.

Max looks outside from time to time. I know he is wondering if his papa, Janis, is still alive in the Small Ghetto which is now just down the road.

At lunchtime Mama puts out a piece of hard sausage that she was saving for our resettlement journey. She cuts it with a blunt knife into four pieces and we each chew on a bit, but the sausage is full of rancid fat and too hard to swallow with ease so in the end we just eat a small piece of bread each and have another cup of water boiled in a saucepan.

"I am so hungry," I say, almost without meaning to say it. Then I flush with shame. There are people outside lying dead in the streets and Omama is missing and I am thinking about myself. It is hard not to think about food, though. Food haunts my thoughts from the moment I wake up until the moment I go to bed with my stomach trying to eat itself and feeling sick.

Mama does not tell me off. She just gives me a weak smile and passes me a small piece of her own bread. I pass it on to Sascha.

There is the sound of sweeping and voices outside so I go to see what is happening.

There are men from the new Small Ghetto in our street, clearing up the bodies and the bloody mess left behind. They tip the bodies onto barrows and carts and wheel them off in the direction of the old Jewish cemetery.

Max strains to see if he can see Janis but there is no sign.

The clearing up of the bodies goes on for most of the evening.

*

It is December the next day.

We wake up stiff with cold but glad to still be alive and together, even though we miss Omama every minute of every day.

Outside the roar of an engine announces the arrival of the SS. They drive through the streets of the ghetto in their open-topped car, inspecting the blood which has frozen in puddles on the white snow. They must be satisfied with what they see because they disappear and the ghetto falls into an uneasy, heavy silence for the rest of the day.

We do not dare venture out, but Max risks it later on and comes back grey in the face. He says that a huge open grave has been dug in the Jewish cemetery. One of the gravediggers told him that seven hundred corpses had been rounded up from the shootings and thrown into this communal trench. No prayers were allowed and nobody was permitted to visit.

Mama shakes her head with a violent gesture, like she is trying to shake off a giant fly.

Then she sits down on the box in the middle of the room and begins to pray again.

There are others still hiding in *Ludzas iela.*

At lunchtime the next day, Mama is delighted when

Zilla and her mother poke their heads around our apartment door.

"Come in!" she says. "Although I am afraid I cannot offer you much to eat."

Mrs Petersohn shakes the snow off her coat and produces a small parcel wrapped in linen and tied with a piece of string.

There are several slices of black bread stuck together in a lump. Zilla puts a beetroot and a couple of carrots with them.

Our faces must have lit up with disbelief and joy because Zilla and her mother burst out laughing and look proud of their food gift.

"The stores are open again, Kristina," says Mrs Petersohn. "And now you do not need your ration cards. Sure, most of the produce is mouldy but there is plenty of it if you have a little money left."

Mama has already got her coat and scarf on and is halfway down the stairs.

"Stay here, I won't be long," she calls back up from below.

She is not just going to buy food. She is going to look for Omama.

*

Mama comes back distraught.

She has not been able to get near the old people's home in the ghetto to find out if Omama is still there. Jews are only allowed to pick up their rations and then go straight back home.

Over our lunch we talk about what has happened.

"I hear that they might have been taken to a new work camp at Salaspils," says Mrs Petersohn. "At least they may get some food if they work."

"Hmm," says Mama. "Or maybe they were taken further east."

"Did you notice though?" says Mrs Petersohn. "Many of the people in the columns were those who were sick and elderly, or very young. How could they work?"

We are silent for a moment. Of course I had noticed that but I don't want to worry Mama any more than she is already worried.

We all know that if you are unable to work, the SS cast you aside like mouldy carrot tops.

"Perhaps we will be marched like that soon," says Mrs Petersohn. "To join the others in the camp. We should try to train up for it. Stay strong. We do not want to be the weak or sick ones on the journey."

There is a general consensus that we should indeed try to build ourselves up a bit for any forthcoming march which might be heading our way.

So for the next couple of days we make a point of walking up and down the stairs and round the rooms, trying to build up the dead muscles in our wasted thighs and calves.

I put my leg up on the window sill and begin to do my dance stretches and warm-ups again, even though I am too weak to do any actual dancing. A lot of the time I am starting to do my dancing in my imagination instead. In my head I am still strong and supple and have hard muscles in my calves. In reality the skin is starting to sag and hang around the backs of my legs.

Max watches me in silence.

His dark eyes start to make me feel strange, but I do not stop. A part of me likes him watching as I bend over my stretched-out leg, showing the arch of my spine and the curve of my buttocks.

At night I have started to think about Max.

It softens the pain of missing Uldis and the anger at what he did to us.

Max is more of a boy than Uldis was but his face is grown-up and serious and I like the way his dark hair flops over one eye and how he looks out for his little sister and passes her the best bits of food. We all do that. It is painful to see a four-year-old child wasting away from hunger.

Mama ventures out to the ghetto store every day and comes back with plentiful amounts of mouldy vegetables but as we are so hungry we wolf them down without complaint.

On the third day of December she comes back inside with a new urgency in her eyes.

"They still need women seamstresses," she pants, throwing down a pile of potatoes and beets so that they tumble off the box and onto the floor. "To work in the city. They will be fed, allowed to stay in the ghetto and not resettled elsewhere!"

She looks at me with her eyes full of hope and confusion.

Then we turn to look at Max and Sascha.

The two of them stand there in silence.

Chapter Seventeen

Love is all about choices.

How do you choose between what is best for one person and what is right for another?

This is the dilemma that Mama has on the evening of 3rd December.

If I had not been involved in the equation too, her choice would have been simple.

"I will go and be resettled in the new work camp," she would have said. "I may find Omama there." But it is not simple. Mama has me to consider too and she is worried about leaving Max and Sascha on their own.

We spend the next half an hour discussing the matter.

"If we take the work as seamstresses here it will only be for a while and we may get food," says Mama. She looks at the stale lump of bread that I am about to eat. It is about the size of a postage stamp. "Then we will be stronger when the time comes for us to go to another camp. On the other hand if we go to the camp sooner, we have more chance of finding Omama."

"What if there is no other camp, anyway?" I say. "We may end up somewhere worse."

Mama looks at me. I can actually see her weighing up the options with a scowl, like the Jewish storekeeper in our ghetto store who weighs up our tiny amounts of rationed sugar on his balancing scales and frowns as he tips it into a tiny bag.

There is no sugar left anywhere now.

"What do you think?" I ask Max. He is home all day with us too at the moment. None of us dare go near the ghetto gates or fence for fear of being shot. Because we are not being called to work at the moment we have very little food left and Mama has only a few pennies of her saved-up money.

Max shrugs. I guess it's not so important to him what happens to my family. He is only concerned with looking after Sascha and finding Janis. There are some holes in the fence to the Small Ghetto but it is under armed guard and too dangerous to risk going through, even though some men from the Small Ghetto have risked it at night-time and come back to our part of the ghetto to see if they can reclaim any of their lost belongings.

In the end it is Max who makes the decision.

"You two go and register as seamstresses," he says to me and Mama. "If you can get work in the city then you can come back here every evening with food for the rest of us."

Mama still looks doubtful but she can see the sense in what he is saying about the food for everybody else.

"Well," she says. "Do up your coat, Hanna. I guess we'd better go and register for work."

By the time Mama and I emerge into the cold and walk to *Mazā Kalna iela* where the registration is taking place, a long line of women and girls has formed there.

"There must be four hundred at least," says Mama. "We will never get to the front of the queue!"

We shuffle our feet in the cold, trying to keep blood flowing around our bodies. I try not to look at the vandalized windows and rooms of the houses around us. Houses which once contained our fellow Jews now stand empty. There are beds and cradles upturned and sometimes lying outside in the yards.

Where have all these people gone?

In one room I can see what is left of an evening meal set on the table, as if the occupants had just stepped outside for a moment.

I eye up the food, wondering if it is worth risking punishment to leave the line and grab it, but Mama can see what I am thinking and mouths a fierce "No!" at me, so I stay in line and swallow down my hunger pangs.

The registration is being taken by the Jewish Council so we feel less scared than usual.

I shift my feet and we move along the queue at the speed of a snail. If I saw a snail now I guess I would rip its shell off and eat it for the protein content.

Mama keeps spotting women she used to know when we lived in our villa.

"She is not a seamstress!" she says with indignation. "Neither is she! What are they doing here?"

Then she falls silent. The answer presents itself in both our heads.

We reach the head of the queue and our names are added to the list of seamstresses.

The Jewish Council member tells us to go back to the apartment, assemble enough food for two days and then meet at this place again at four o'clock in the afternoon.

Mama frowns.

"Two days?" she says. "I thought we were going to

work in the city every day. Won't they give us food there?"

The Jewish Council lady raises her eyebrows at Mama and gestures her to move aside so that the next woman can register.

Mama is very quiet on the way back round the corner to *Ludzas iela.*

Just before four o'clock we pick up our knapsacks and say goodbye to Max and Sascha.

I can tell that Max is worried about being left with only a tiny child for company, from the way he keeps glancing at his little sister. I guess it won't be exactly ideal, but we are hoping it won't be for very long.

Mama tries to make our goodbye just the same as usual.

"Do not forget to peel the carrots," she says, strictly. "We will need to eat when we return."

Max nods. Then he takes my arm and holds me back.

"Your mama is not too well," he whispers. "Look after her."

My heart sinks at his mention of Mama's health. I have been trying not to notice her grey skin and the barking sound of her cough. But Mama is already going downstairs and I don't much feel like getting lost outside in the crowded street.

I turn to go but he has not yet finished.

"And Hanna? Be proud of who you are," he says. "Your blood. It is nothing to be ashamed of."

I nod, surprised. Max never says things like this. He sounds about eighty years old.

"I'll remember," I say. "But we'll be back later."

Then I start to leave but something makes me dart back and kiss his cheek. I can feel the bone underneath the skin.

I follow my mother out of the apartment and into the street outside.

We cross almost the entire city.

There are about three hundred women, some barely more than young girls. We all wear two yellow stars and many of us have our greasy, unkempt hair shoved into dark headscarves as we have long since been banned from wearing hats.

We pass several workshops and barracks belonging to the German army and each time I think that we are going to be told to stop and assigned a new workplace but we just keep going.

I feel as if I am an intruder on the streets of my own city. It is a shock to see Latvian men and women in fur coats and warm hats going about their business as if nothing has happened.

Some of them stare at us from the sidewalk but avert their eyes when we try to make eye contact with them.

One woman makes the sign of the cross and lowers her head.

I stare, confused. We are Jews, so we do not make the sign of the cross. The woman is hurrying away now, muttering to herself.

I want to ask Mama where she thinks we might be going but even a single sentence uttered out of turn and we are likely to be beaten around the head with a gun so I keep quiet.

After nearly an hour of walking we approach the Brasa railway station just outside Rīga. It is a mass of train tracks and grim industrial buildings. Next to it rises up a dark brown brick building with strange pointed chimneys and arched glass windows covered in black bars. There are small square buildings raised up all around it, from where uniformed guards keep watch at the top of tall ladders.

We are marched through an electric gate into the courtyard of this building.

A scene of chaos greets our eyes.

There are upturned chairs tossed about on the ground

and stinking mattresses piled up in the corner. Scattered around are shoes and items of clothing, all battered and worn. Some of the shoes have no laces. By the damp brick wall lie piles of empty bags and suitcases, jutting out at odd angles.

I grip on to Mama's arm.

She is trying not to cough. Her shoulders are shaking with the effort.

"What is this?" I manage to whisper.

A couple of women from our group turn round and glare at me. The penalty for speaking is too high for all us, but I have to know.

"Merciful God," says my mother, clutching at her throat. "They have not brought us to work. They have brought us to prison."

As if on cue, a couple of guards appear.

"Well," says one of them with a slow smile. "Aren't you just the daughters of fortune?"

I guess he is being sarcastic. I can't see anything very lucky about being taken to the Central Prison. All my life Mama warned me to stay well away from this place and now I am actually inside it I can see why.

The guards start to push us towards a dingy flight of concrete stairs. There is very little light, so the women stumble and clutch one another.

I try to hold Mama up by her arm and to guide her as best I can.

We emerge into a dark, stuffy rooftop space and are pushed in so hard that some women fall to the floor with cries of pain or indignation. The floor is already crowded from wall to wall with women sitting huddled in the semi-dark. There is one window but boards are nailed over the glass so that there are only tiny slits about the width of three fingers.

There is a clank as the heavy metal door slams behind us.

I go over and try to look down to the ground and see what is going on but the slits have been arranged in such a way that I can only look to the sky and not downwards.

We are isolated. Cut off from the outside world.

I turn round. About five hundred women crouch, lie or stand in this one attic.

Many of them are in tears.

We are kept in the attic for one night and most of the next day.

The air up here stinks.

I have taken to pulling my jacket collar up over my

nose. I prefer the odour of my own unwashed skin to that of everybody else.

We have no toilet up here other than a bucket in the corner of the room and that fills up almost straight away.

No guards or police come in again but from time to time the door opens and another load of women are shoved onto the floor to join us.

Up here with all the women it becomes unimportant who knows who or lived where or wore what in our previous lives.

Up here we all band together to try to survive.

The food we brought in our knapsacks is pooled. We share it with those who are weaker or older than us. Nobody brings us any water so it is difficult to force hard dry lumps of bread down our throats but we try.

Mama's cough is getting worse. It is damp and fetid up here and the lack of fresh air is making everybody feel ill. We sleep half-propped-up against one another, our limbs sore from the hard floor.

On the second day a guard bursts in and takes us by surprise. We are lying in apathetic heaps on the floor and up against the wall, crammed in like the Baltic sardines that Omama loves so much and smelling twice as bad.

"Fifty volunteers to go downstairs!" shouts the guard.

Mama and I look at one another. In a flash we are by the door.

"It cannot be worse," Mama whispers.

In fact, it is not much better. We are moved to a basement which is just as crowded as our attic. The floor is freezing cold and there is only one tiny window up in a corner and protected by thick black steel bars.

A Latvian prison guard is stationed outside this cell. He watches us through a peephole in the door. I don't know what he expects us to do. We can hardly rebel, crammed in like this and weak from lack of food and sleep.

They do not give us any water here either and our food is gone.

There is a long table in the middle of the room and I manage to help Mama onto it to sleep that night because the floor is too cold and damp.

I do not sleep. I stand up all night underneath the tiny window, looking at the chink of sky. I tell myself that as long as I can see the outside I will be all right. I always feel better when I can see the open sky.

Little thoughts weave themselves through my tired brain. Papa, Omama, Uldis, Velna, Uncle Georgs. The same five faces, over and over. I miss them all in different ways.

The pain of losing Omama is the freshest pain.

But still I miss Papa. He's like the rock on which the rest of my life was grown. I wonder if he's out there now, looking up at the same sky and worrying about me and Mama?

"I will find you," I whisper under my breath. "Or at least, I will try."

Behind me a woman who has been crying in pain all night, drops to the floor like a stone.

In the morning a harsh grey light streams through the tiny window.

The women wake up and begin to try and groom themselves a little, which is difficult with no proper light, no water, no clean clothes, combs or facecloths.

Another man bursts in. He is the prison supervisor, he announces. He has come to collect our reports.

There is a panic as the women look at one another and back at the man.

"We have not got a report," ventures one of them, a woman with a thin fox-like face and straggly black hair escaping from her headscarf.

The guard slaps her so hard that she falls against the wall and then to the floor where she lies stunned.

None of us dare go to her.

"You lazy Jewesses!" shouts the guard. "Even shooting is too good for you!"

Then he slams the metal door and leaves us reeling, our hearts pounding.

We are shut in this room for two whole days.

Mama and I lie together on the edge of the table at night and although we do not speak, I know that we are both thinking about the same things.

We dream of Omama and of our old life in the villa with Papa and the cherry trees in the garden.

I even wish I was back in the ghetto.

All things are relative. At least there we only had six of us to worry about and we had our own apartment even though it was cold and basic.

When I think of my grandmother and the way she was dragged away from us, a painful lump comes up in my throat and my eyes prick with what would be tears only my body seems to have dried up from lack of water and no tears will come.

If they did, I would probably try to drink them.

After two days the lock on the door turns and the supervisor comes in again.

"All out!" he shouts. "Quick."

The women rise up like a mass of flapping frightened pigeons. Some of them start to scream.

"My God," shouts one. "We are all going to be shot."

I go dizzy when she says this. I hold on to Mama and she strokes my oily plaits and shakes her head at me, although how she can possibly know what is going to happen to us, beats me.

"They would have done it by now," Mama whispers. "We must stay calm. Follow me, do what I do. All right?"

I nod.

We are being taken back out into the prison courtyard where we first began this ordeal.

There is even more chaos out there now. There is so much furniture strewn about with the mattresses and shoes that we can find very little space to stand on the ground.

The guards form us into one of the usual columns and start marching us into a large hallway. We blink in pain at the light streaming through the windows. This is some sort of administration building. By the huge arched windows at the end sit a line of SS officers in their military uniforms.

They are gesturing some women to the right and others to the left.

There is no way of telling which of these directions is good and which is bad.

We wait our turn in the queue and then Mama and I stand, trembling, in front of the officers.

There is one woman in front of us. I recognize her from our old life in *Skārņu iela*. Mrs Muris. She lived in our apartment block.

I am pretty sure she is not a seamstress.

The German officer barks something at her and then gestures her to the left.

"Thank God. I am going back to the ghetto," the woman mutters.

This tells me that whatever I do, I must somehow get sent to the left-hand side. Now that there seem to be no signs of us being sent to work as seamstresses in the city, the best option must be to get sent back to *Ludzas iela* and be reunited with Max and Sascha.

Mama has obviously come to the same conclusion as she raises her eyebrows at me and tilts her head towards the left with a tiny movement that only I can see.

"Put samples of your work here," says the German officer. He looks up at me with cold blue eyes.

Mama knows what to do. In her knapsack she has samples of her sewing work but instead of pulling out the exquisite examples of bugle beading and intricate embroidery, she instead lays out some plain coloured squares with uneven stitching. I realize that they are the pieces she got me to practise on when we still lived in *Skārņu iela* and despite everything I bite back a smile.

"Some of this is my daughter's work," she says, putting down another two pieces of material.

I hold my breath.

There is an endless silence whilst the officer looks at the bad samples. He then looks me in the eye for what feels like for ever and a day.

Then with a tiny flick of his forefinger he gestures us to the left.

We stand with the growing group of women and clutch one another's hands.

There are beads of sweat on Mama's forehead and she looks grey but she allows me the tiniest of sideways smiles and squeezes my hand.

Perhaps we are the daughters of fortune after all.

We are going back to the ghetto.

We survive to fight another day.

Chapter Eighteen

We are kept for one last night in the crowded basement of the Central Prison.

Mama works out the date.

She has been trying to keep track of the days. It is difficult without a watch and the nights and days seem to be one long continuation of physical and mental anguish. We never have anything to eat and are rarely given water. In these conditions it is hard to tell whether one hour has passed, let alone a day.

But Mama keeps track.

"It gives me something to do," she says with a cough. Her cough has got far worse in the dank atmosphere of our prison accommodation. I asked one of the guards if she could have some medicine but I was met with a glare and a laugh of displeasure.

"You are Jewesses," he said. "We don't owe you anything."

When we finally get back to *Ludzas iela* I will ask Max to go out and see if he can get some cough medicine for Mama.

Until then I have to watch my mother retch and cough her guts up onto the rough grey asphalt floor of the prison.

It is 6th December, Mama says.

We are ordered out of the attic and down into the courtyard where we are formed into columns five women wide.

Then with our usual accompaniment of stone-faced Latvian guards we are marched out of the great gates of the prison and alongside the railway track.

"We are going back!" I whisper to Mama as we retrace the route we came on a few short days ago. It feels like years.

We pass through the centre of town again. As before, Latvians give us looks of pity. Some of them give us looks of astonishment and vague smiles. I can't work out why. It is almost as if they never expected to see us again. One or two even dare a nod or a small wave. Others ignore us and hurry past with their heads bent against the biting sleet and icy winds. I think of Velna and the air takes on a heavy grey chill. *Dirty Jew.* That's what those people are thinking about me.

A couple of hundred or so of us are marched back towards the Maskavas area of town and the ghetto. Some of the women are so weak that they collapse during the hour-long walk.

Their bodies are shoved to the side of the road by the SS and left there, part-disappearing under the new flurry of snow.

I start to see the streets of the ghetto up ahead.

I clutch Mama's arm, dizzy with relief. We will be back in our grotty apartment on *Ludzas iela* soon and I will be able to see Max and Sascha.

When we get to number 29 I almost hurl myself up the stairs. Part of me is hoping that Omama will have somehow escaped the old people's home or the resettlement column and be waiting up here with open arms, but a larger part of me knows that this won't be true.

At least Max will still be here waiting for us.

I burst into the main room of the apartment with a smile upon my face.

A tiny whimper greets me.

Sascha is curled up in the corner of the room underneath a blanket. Her tufts of hair are poking out of the top.

There is no sign of Max.

He's gone.

We can't get much sense out of Sascha.

We ask her as many questions as we can but she is fraught with hunger and anxiety and in the end Mama just makes a thin soup out of old vegetables, tucks her up and sings her some old nursery rhymes until Sascha's eyes close and she lies immobile on her thin mattress.

I hope that Max has been taken away to work in the Small Ghetto.

I spend the evening straining my eyes to look out of the window while Mama finds what she can to eat. I can see some of the Small Ghetto from here and my eyes latch on to every man and boy I see in a cap in case they are Max or Janis but I just can't tell from up here and it is too dangerous to go out and wander the streets.

My heart aches with longing for my grandmother. And there's another thing. I really miss Max, with a sharp new pain I haven't experienced before. I keep calling up his dark hair and brown eyes and trying to imagine that he is going to come back and give me his rare shy smile.

Mama and I huddle around our old box-table which still sits in the middle of the room. We try not to talk about Omama but her presence is everywhere, large and vibrant for such a small, wrinkled old lady.

The next morning I wake from a nightmare in which Uldis finds me and locks me inside a house in the countryside and forces me to have four blond children whose Jewish blood is diluted until they become pure Aryan.

"Fat chance," I say, waking on the hard floor with a pounding headache and sore eyes.

"What?" says Mama. She has obviously been awake for a while because she is sitting with her arms around her knees, watching me.

"I dreamed of Uldis," I say, before I become properly awake. I watch Mama's face change into a hard shell.

"That traitor," she says. "It is because of him that we are here."

I shake my head.

"No," I say in a small voice. "It is because of me that we are here."

Mama's face fills with pain and love.

"Don't ever think that, Hanna," she says. "He persuaded the secret out of you. As far as I am concerned, it is his fault and his fault alone."

How could I have been so stupid as to betray my family's hiding place?

I have made all this happen. It is because of me that Omama has been taken away.

The guilt is eating me alive, like worms inside an apple.

What I wouldn't give for an apple right now.

We wait for the command to get back to work.

We are sure that we will have to work again for our measly rations of food and our cold and lice-ridden lodgings.

The command never comes.

The ghetto is freezing.

The sky refuses to get light.

When I go out to queue for rations I can see that most of the houses which were once crammed full of Jews sharing apartments together are empty, abandoned by their residents in a hurry on the November night when I last saw my Omama.

The ghetto is very quiet. Too quiet.

Only two days after we have returned to our apartment a new order is issued. It says that all able-bodied men remaining in the Large Ghetto must instead report to the

Small Ghetto and that the rest of the population will be "moved".

Mama and I hold hands and can't speak. Sascha is in the room with us and is watching our every move with her big, haunted eyes. There is stuff we need to say but we can't say it in front of her. We wait until she has been put to bed on the mattress in the corner of the room. Mama tucks the thin, rotting blanket over her and tries to sing a bedtime song, but her voice keeps cracking with fear, tiredness and emotion so in the end I take over and sing "Raisins and Almonds" in a thin, wobbling voice that sounds nothing like the one I used to have at our villa.

When Sascha is asleep for her afternoon nap, Mama and I chew on one of the endless lumps of stale hard bread that have become our life. Then she takes my hand again and looks into my face.

"We cannot trust them any more," she says. "They lied about the work in the city and instead took us to the prison. They said that Omama was in the old people's home but nobody has heard of her or seen her since. We have had no proof that all those people ever reached a camp."

She stops for a moment. We are both trying not to cry. The spectre of my bad-tempered, loving old grandmother looms large between us, waving her stick and crowing in her sharp voice.

"So this 'resettlement' notice is a sham, too," says Mama. "There's no point pretending otherwise."

I nod. I have known this since the order went up. I can hear the cries and panicky voices of the remaining residents of our ghetto. We have all seen too much to pretend that this news is anything other than the worst possible.

Even so, I still have a small bead of hope inside me.

Maybe they will take us to a work camp after all.

Maybe they still need seamstresses somewhere.

Maybe the war will end and we will be freed.

I see Papa's face, strong and kind with his eyes flashing love and compassion.

I promised him I would look after Mama for as long as we both lived.

I grip her hand.

"We will be together, Mama," I say. "I won't let go of your hand. I promise. Whatever happens, we will be together. I have decided!"

Mama smiles a little at my catchphrase but she can't speak. Her fingers feel like chicken bones in my hand. But she nods, her lip trembling. Her eyes speak of love and loss and torment.

On the other side of the room, Sascha throws her blanket off, restless and in tears.

I sing her another song and try to stem the flow of my own.

The ghetto is dark by six.

A couple more hours pass.

Mama and I are ready.

We have been listening to shooting all around the ghetto for several hours now and we have heard the commands shouted into the darkness for people to leave their lodgings.

We have our small knapsacks crammed with as much food and as many blankets and items of clothing as we can stuff in. We have dressed Sascha in the warmest clothes we possess and put a little knitted bonnet on her head.

The order comes from the streets.

"Out! Out!" shout the Latvian policemen. "All ghetto inhabitants must leave their buildings immediately!"

I take Mama's hand and Mama offers her other hand to Sascha.

Mama looks at me.

"Ready?" she says.

"Ready," I say.

Then we go downstairs to meet our fate.

Chapter Nineteen

We are pushed into columns of people, five abreast.

The men are mostly old. No use as workers.

The women are either elderly or young mothers with tiny, terrified children.

This is the same thing I saw from the windows of our apartment on the day Omama was taken from us. The same terrified mass of people whipped into orderly lines. The same desperate clutching of bags and packages to chests. The same mixture of facial expressions – fear, terror, sadness, blankness, impassiveness and even acceptance on the faces of some of the more elderly residents of the ghetto. It is like they have given up already.

I stand in line with Mama and Sascha and although a nasty sick feeling has got me in the pit of my stomach

I remind myself of Papa's face and I think: *I will not give up.*

We stand for an hour. It is cold, but there is no snow.

A Latvian policeman says that the elderly men and women and the mothers with children are being treated to a special sleigh so that they do not have to walk. These people are to form a separate column.

Mama catches my eye and as if of one mind we push Sascha between ourselves and cover her with our coats. Then we watch as other mothers holding tiny children by the hand and babies in their arms, walk towards the column to wait for their special sleigh.

"May God protect them," whispers Mama.

The order is given for our column to start moving.

Each crack of the whip pushes us further forward. Sometimes the police use guns instead.

We pass out of *Ludzas iela* and into *Līksnas iela.*

On the junction of these two streets is an SS man. He is holding a gun and a wooden club.

"Drop your packages here!" he commands, as we straggle by.

People begin to shed their bags and packets with looks of stunned disbelief.

I drop mine straight away. There seems little point in arguing with an armed member of the SS. Mama drops hers too, with an anguished look at Sascha. We have packed bread and a precious bottle of milk for her in our bags.

A woman who is either brave or stupid runs up to the SS man. She throws herself at his feet.

"Please," she begs. "I have food for my children with me. Let me keep some of it!"

"You don't need to worry about food where you are going," says the SS man with a sneer. He uses the butt of his gun to hit the woman across the cheek. We hear the crack of bone and watch as she staggers back into line, clutching her face.

We are being marched past the old Jewish cemetery.

I remember Omama's half-joke about how convenient our new lodgings were. A shudder of ice passes up my spine.

The road is slippery. Snow has melted during the night and made the pavements treacherous underfoot. I help Mama stay upright and together we are almost lifting Sascha's feet off the ground so that she does not fall or worse, get trampled by the column.

When I glance back, the column is so long that I cannot see the end of it. There must be thousands of us here, being whipped and shouted towards who-knows-what.

We are now on the main *Maskavas iela.* The faint light of dawn is starting to appear.

Maybe the SS are panicking about the ordinary people of Rīga who will soon be using this road to go to their shops and offices. Maybe they haven't allowed enough time to get us all to our destination, for they start to shout at us to go faster. Some people cannot. They fall to the side of the road and lie there, motionless and forgotten. If they are still alive they are finished off with a brief shot to the head.

We stumble on for several more kilometres.

Then I recognize the Rumbula railway station.

Mama and Papa used to bring me here when I was a little girl. We would walk from the station to the nearby forest and have a picnic amidst the trees.

I see this image as if I am looking into somebody else's past and not my own. How can that fat little girl with the pigtails and chubby red cheeks rolling on a blanket be the same person I am today? Now I can hardly straighten my legs. Every bone in my body hurts. My teeth have become grey and loose from lack of brushing and my hair is starting to fall out from never having enough to eat.

Mama was so pretty. I can see her handing out the fresh rolls and smoked fish that she brought on our picnics. She bends over the food, her dark hair thick and lush and her lips full and red.

I glance sideways at Mama.

She looks like an old woman. She looks older now than Omama.

A terrible fear rips through me.

For the first time I realize that my mother is weak and vulnerable.

She is not a person to the Nazis. She is just another frail, starving Jew, cluttering up land that they want for themselves.

I look down at Sascha, stumbling along on her short pencil-legs between Mama and myself and my heart contracts.

Surely they must be able to spare the children?

I am brought back to the present with a jolt.

I can hear shooting.

This is not the occasional gunshot. No. This is the *ack-ack-ack* of a continual motion.

The harsh sound of dogs barking grows louder as we approach the forest.

I begin to shiver. Panic is rising up in me now and I get an overpowering urge to scream and break free, run in the opposite direction.

But we are surrounded by both SS and Latvian police now, along with their snarling, red-eyed dogs.

Mama begins to pray. I mouth the words with her in

silence, trying to focus on them so that I don't give in to my urge to try and run.

We are whipped and beaten towards a large box at the edge of the forest.

A soldier of the SS yells at us to remove our jewellery and put it along with any valuables into this box.

People obey meekly, like sheep.

The gold and silver flows into the box and onto the ground. I see the soldier pick up the fallen pieces and shove some of them into his pocket. He does this in full view of everybody, with an insolent grin.

What are you Jews going to do about it?

That's what his expression says.

We are herded on ahead. A Latvian policeman orders us to remove our coats and throw them onto a huge pile which is growing in a pyramid nearby.

Mama removes Sascha's little coat with shaking hands, fumbling at the buttons.

Sascha begins to wail. Mama shoots me a look of anguish. I crouch down and put my hand over Sascha's mouth so that Mama can finish the unbuttoning.

"Be a good girl," I say. "We will be staying with you, don't worry."

It is all I can think of to say. I cannot lie and say that everything will be all right.

The sound of guns becomes louder by the second.

We are pushed, shivering, towards another area where we are commanded to remove all our clothes and just keep on our underclothes.

There is no point refusing. We are done for, either way.

A group of young Jewish women take the clothes and sort them into piles. They do not look at us once. They have guns in their backs and no expressions on their thin faces.

There is no longer any deception, any faint hope that things will be all right or that we are going to a work camp.

The shots, the screams, the shivering, the terror.

Here, now, right in front of us.

Mama and I squeeze Sascha's thin little hands as tightly as we can.

A part of me watches all this from above, detached and furious.

I can hardly believe that my short life is soon to be over in this way.

The cold bites into our bare flesh.

I am pushed on, shivering in my white knickers and vest, clinging to Mama and Sascha, who are also in their thin underclothes.

All around us women, children and old people are

screaming, crying and praying. It is a mass of anguished sound, like thousands of trapped and wounded animals all baying for help.

We are forced forwards for a short while longer and then stopped with an abrupt command of "Halt!" from the soldiers.

And then I see it.

The pit.

It is almost full to the brim with bodies. Some of them are still. Others seem to be moving.

My eyes try to adjust to what I am seeing. The clack of the guns is deafening and people are being shoved into the pit so fast that they almost seem to blur.

"Oh my God," Mama cries, gripping my arm. "Hanna, Hanna. It is the end."

Tears begin to pour down my face.

In a flash I understand what is happening.

The Jews are being shot in the head where they lie in the pit. Then the next line of Jews is forced to lie, packed like Omama's Baltic sardines, on top of the dead bodies. These living people are then killed in the same manner.

People are running and jumping down into the pits. It is like they are pleased to get in there, but I know this is not the case. It is just that you cannot disobey the order of the SS and their dogs and guns.

I hold Mama's hand so tight that I am sure they can never break us up.

"I love you," I say to my mother.

"Not as much as I love you," says Mama. "I am proud to have been your mother."

"Do you forgive me?" I say, panic rising in my heart. I have to know. I can't go to my death not knowing.

"Nothing to forgive," says Mama.

We are ripped apart by the guards.

"NO!" I scream. "Mama! Don't leave me!"

Sascha and Mama run in front of me, down into the pit.

Everything seems to slow down. I see every exaggerated detail of their climb onto the dead bodies. The way that Mama's knees fail to bend properly and she half-stumbles and lands on her back on top of the corpses. The way that Sascha does a tumbling head-over-heels into the grave, as if she is on a rubber mat in the school gymnasium.

I make to run after them and take my place by their side but I am halted by a gun in my chest.

They have enough people in that row.

And so, standing at the edge of that pit, I am forced to watch my mother and Sascha die.

Two shots. They seem louder than all the rest.

Mama gives one small jerk and then lies still.

But Sascha flies up into the air like a rag doll in white underwear before flopping back down again.

My screams fall on empty ears.

Everybody here is screaming.

I am alone.

"Into the pit!" commands the Latvian policeman standing next to me.

I start to stumble towards the pit, towards the dead bodies of Mama and Sascha.

I lie down on top of their corpses. I can feel the knees, knuckles and noses of the dead, poking into my back. I retch over and over but nothing comes out.

In my head I offer up my final prayers to God. I ask Him to find Papa and send him back to Rīga safely, so that at least one of our family might survive this war.

I ask Him for strength to face my final moments on this earth and I even manage to thank Him for all the good things I used to have in my life.

I lie and wait for my bullet. I squeeze shut my eyes and clench my teeth, ready for the impact.

And then He listens.

God listens.

There is a momentary uproar elsewhere in the forest. It is loud enough to distract the four marksmen who stand with their guns, one on each corner of the death pit.

I half open my eyes.

Their heads are turned for maybe five seconds.

I burrow right underneath the body of my mother. She is still warm.

Then I hold my breath with my mouth full of white cotton drawers. I pray like I have never prayed before.

Don't see me. Please don't see me.

More people are driven into the pit and lie down on top of Mama and Sascha.

I am squashed under the weight of the new people. They are all praying and muttering and crying to God. I can smell them – dirty clothes, unwashed bodies and hair, the smell of disease and starvation.

I hold my breath a little. I keep on praying and picturing the face of my papa.

The shooting starts again and the people on top of me jerk upwards and then are still. They grow heavier.

I pray to God that they are the last row of people to be put in this pit.

Blood begins to ooze downwards onto my face and arms but I daren't move.

The breath is being squeezed out of me by the weight of the bodies above me. Mama is as light as a feather but the people on top of her are squashing us right down.

I start to feel dizzy from lack of air. I use my hand to

make a cup around my mouth and I try to breathe in and out in slow, measured breaths.

The noise of the guns has stopped.

There are other noises – engines revving up, men shouting and laughing, dogs barking.

Then a new substance begins to filter down to where I am lying.

It feels like sand. But it has a sharp smell and a burning feel. My face and eyes begin to get sore and blister so I shut my eyes tight and press my face into Mama's back. I think of when she was pregnant with me. I must have been pressed up against it from the other side, safe inside the womb.

"Mama," I whisper, tears mixing with the burning substance in my eyes. The tears cool them a little.

A new weight begins to press down on me. I can't think what it is, but then I strain my ears and think that I can hear the sound of shovels. Something thumps on top of the bodies and tiny lumps of grit and mud work their way down onto my face and body.

I panic.

Earth. They are closing the grave.

I am to be buried alive.

*

It is very dark.

I have no idea how long I have lain here.

My mouth is full of earth and insects. Soil chokes the back of my throat. It is steeped in the blood of the victims. I can taste the metal tang. I retch over and over. My nose is full of the damp earthiness of the forest mixed with the smell of bodies.

I am running out of oxygen. I feel weak from having no air to breathe and from the relentless weight of the bodies and the earth on top of me.

Disjointed thoughts pass through my head.

I think:

This is what it is like underneath trees, all the time.

I wonder if any of my bones have broken?

Am I really down here? Still alive? Or am I dead?

Later on, as the pressure on my chest increases and I feel weaker:

This is how Omama died.

She was so tiny and thin. She'd have never stood a chance.

Neither would Mama or Sascha. They had lost all their fight.

Then I think:

But I am still here, thinking stuff through. So I must be alive, right?

And if I'm alive, I might be able to work out what to do.

I have no indecision at all now. I know that I have to survive this. Not just to find Papa, but to tell other people what has happened to the Jews of Rīga.

"I need to get out of here," I say into the dark earth.

My mouth is crammed with the stuff.

I lie for a while longer, to make sure that I have the best chance.

I count the seconds and minutes in my head and try to get to another hour.

Then I summon up all my mental energy and focus it into my arms.

They are thin and weaker than they used to be and I am numb from lying still for so long, but I have a plan.

I have never forgotten my ballet moves. Even when I couldn't physically do them in the ghetto I would run through them in my head when I couldn't sleep at night.

One of the first things we were taught was how to do our five basic arm positions.

I am lying down rather than standing up. But I take the deepest breath that I can and try to bring my arms in front of me. Then I push my arms away from one another into second position. I am aware that I am pushing my arms into the bodies of dead people but I pretend that I am in the swimming pool in the days before Jews got banned and that I am pushing my arms against the weight of the water. Then with a superhuman effort I heave one arm up over my head into fourth position and with it I manage to shift Mama's body a little, just enough to push my arm a little higher into the earth above. My other arm goes up to join it and I stay in fifth position until my arms start to shake and tremble and I have to rest.

I wait until I can summon up a little strength.

Then I repeat the whole sequence again.

All the time I try to ignore the horror of what I am pushing against and I just imagine myself in that pool, parting the current with my arms. After what seems like a lifetime I have positioned myself on top of Mama's body rather than underneath it.

I lie there for a moment, gasping for breath with silent tears adding to the mix of tastes in the back of my mouth.

I am glad I cannot see anything.

But I feel her there. I say:

"Goodbye, Mama. I love you."

I don't want to leave her. But I have to get out of here.

With another couple of mighty pushes I start to work my way past the next row of bodies.

*

My head hits the fresh air what seems like years later.

I gulp and cough and wipe the soil and the stinging substance off my eyes and face.

I stand with my body still submerged in the pit and my head peeking out of it for quite some time.

I use my eyes to look left and right. I keep my head motionless. I do not know who might still be in this forest and what they are planning to do.

I can't tell whether the faint light in the forest is the beginning of another day or the end of the previous one. I don't know how long I have been lying in this ghastly pit.

I wait a while longer, straining my ears to pick up even the slightest noise.

There is nothing, save the rustle of leaves, the distant sound of trains and traffic and some odd humming noise which I can't place.

I can't even hear any birds.

The birds won't sing at Rumbula.

I heave myself right up out of that grave.

I stand on the edge of the pit and look down at it.

The humming noise increases.

My stomach lurches with shock.

The Latvian soldiers have filled in the grave with earth but they must have failed to aim their shots as accurately as it seemed.

The earth is singing.

Moans and cries filter their way up into the cold air.

The earth is moving.

Red, oozing, shifting.

The full horror of what has happened hits me harder than the butt of a soldier's rifle.

I drop to my knees on the edge of the grave.

I call "Hello?" in a wavering voice. "Can I help anyone? I am a Jew."

Then I call again, as loudly as I dare.

But nobody can hear me. They must have been buried lower down.

Sobbing, I turn away.

My body is jerking and buckling with the cold.

I am still dressed only in my underwear.

I look around. I see the mountain of clothes, sorted into piles but not yet taken away.

I scuttle over, all the time looking around the forest. I am very nervous of soldiers arriving back unexpectedly.

I grab clothes from the pile. I choose women's clothing but some instinct tells me to cover them up with men's. I put on an oversized white shirt and a long black pullover, a pair of men's grey trousers. I find the pile of coats further back in the forest and I choose the thickest I can find in the darkest colours. Then I shove my hair up into a flat grey cap.

I am warm.

But I am not safe.

And I am alone.

No mother.

No grandmother.

Nobody.

I run deeper into the forest as quickly as I can, trying not to make much noise on the twigs and leaves underfoot. I find a tree with a wide trunk and squash myself up behind it.

Then I wait.

Chapter Twenty

I SPEND THE NEXT FEW HOURS pressed up against the tree with my chin on my knees and my arms wrapped around them.

The sun is starting to rise so I know it is the dawn of a new day.

I don't have long to sit here.

I am shivering from shock and cold and each time I start to think about Mama I try to push the thought aside. I am not ready to accept the full horror of what has just happened to me.

My brain runs feverishly through a list of possibilities.

I can't go back to the old town to try and find somewhere to sleep. That much is clear. I will be shot or, at best, allowed one night sleeping rough before somebody recognizes me as a Jew and reports me to the authorities.

I can't hide out in this forest for long. The SS might be planning to bring more people here to kill.

I can't walk out of the forest and ask anybody for help. They might be a Jew-hater.

Mama! my soul cries out in pain.

There is nobody left to help me.

Nobody.

Then it is as if a light shines into my brain.

Yes.

There is.

I have not seen him for some time but if he was taken away to work in the Small Ghetto then there is a chance that I will find him there. I might even find his father, too.

I must get back somehow to the Small Ghetto and find Max! He will help me. I am sure of it.

My heart gives a little skip of nervousness.

I stand up, ready to find my way out of the forest. Then I remember that it is now daylight.

I sit down again.

I look around.

I have spent a long time lying under the dark ground and I don't much want to do it again but this is the only way I might get out of here alive.

With weak arms I manage to dig myself a pit, just big enough so that I can lie inside it and cover myself with leaves and earth. I pray to God that no SS sniffer dogs will come to this part of the forest in the next few hours.

I am starving. I pick a few berries and some soft leaves and stuff them into my mouth, not caring that in a few hours I will probably have the worst cramps of my life. My stomach has shrunk so much that even a few bits of unripe fruit will have a bad effect.

Then I crawl inside my tiny pit, shut out the light and wait.

I have to judge the amount of time gone by without being able to see much sky.

There's a tiny crack in the leaves I've covered myself with. I peer up through it and watch as the sun rises. Then I try to sleep for a while. When I wake up the sun has started to lower again. As far as I can make out, it must be about four or five o'clock in the afternoon.

I push myself out of the ground and sit still for a moment.

I listen. I sharpen my ears and strain for any sound.

Nothing.

The humming has stopped.

I stand up and brush my strange men's clothing free of earth and leaves.

Then I leave this forest of Hell.

It takes me a while to get my bearings as I go.

I'm weak from lack of food and still in shock.

As I walk in what I hope is the direction of *Maskavas iela* I think of this time last year. I can't believe that the only thing I had to worry about back then was how long it would take me to save up for new ballet shoes and whether I could get a new dress too.

This time last year, Mama, Papa and I were still living in the beautiful villa with the cherry trees. I was studying at the ballet school and spending most of my time trying to look pretty for Uldis.

Just the thought of his name makes me feel sick.

Traitor.

The word is spat out in Omama's voice, not my own.

Tears rise up in my eyes but I trudge on.

The only thing which matters now is finding a friend.

I need to stay alive.

In case Papa is still out there somewhere.

*

There is no use going straight to the ghetto.

If I did that I would face the Latvian policemen on the gate and if they asked me to remove my cap they'd be sure to realize that I was left over from the forest massacre. They would wonder what on earth I was doing on the other side of the gates and probably shoot me on sight.

I have ripped off the yellow stars from my borrowed clothes. I have no fear of doing that now. It is not about being Jewish any more. It has gone beyond that. It is about being alive or being dead. I pull the cap tighter over my hair and button up my oversized coat. I roll up the legs of the man's trousers a little bit to stop them flapping around my ankles.

Then I lower my head and walk along the pavements. Even this feels odd after so many months spent walking in the gutter, but I mustn't be suspected as a Jew.

I am reaching the old part of town. It is nearly dark.

I make my way across the town to *Jelgavas iela*. It takes me a long time, because the streets look different at night and I am not thinking straight.

It's a long shot. I don't even know if they are still working there.

But after hiding behind a wall of the building next door for what seems like eternity, I see the lights in the factory window start to blink off like tired eyelids.

I wait.

A line of figures in dark coats assembles outside.

I hear the usual crack of whips and the shouts of the Latvian policemen.

The figures shuffle into columns and are given the order to start walking.

I am in the right place.

I wait until the line has reached where I am hiding and then I slip out from behind the wall and am into the line of people before anybody has had a chance to notice.

I keep my head down and trudge along with the rest of the men.

The ground underneath is slippery and treacherous but I don't care.

My heart is pounding hard and I can hardly believe what I've done.

I've done it. I've joined a work detail. I am going back to the Small Ghetto.

I am still alive.

The walk back to the ghetto takes just over half an hour.

I am jostled against the man next to me as I walk along but I take care not to look him in the face.

The walk is silent and grim.

The men walking with me are little more than skeletons wearing dark coats. Even in the gloom of the evening I catch glimpses when we pass near a street light. I can see their profiles of bone and skin and little else. There is a smell of decay and unwashed bodies and a feeling of – what?

Acceptance?

Resignation?

Lack of hope?

I am not sure. But whatever it is it comes off in droves from these silent men as they are marched back towards their foodless homes.

I allow myself to be jostled and pushed back with them. My legs feel weak and my stomach aches from the raw fruit I ate earlier. I am going back to – what? No Mama, no Omama, no Sascha and no future. For the first time I think: *It might be easier just to fall over into the gutter and die.*

Then I push the thought aside.

Papa's face looms up in front of me. My memory of him is a little less clear. I can't quite get the exact shape of his face and for the first time I doubt the colour of his eyes. But the expression in them is still strong and clear.

Be strong, my little dancing girl.

That's what he's always telling me.

And I promised.

I failed to keep my other promise – to look after Mama. So I have to keep this one.

So I take a shaky breath of the cold night air and continue to march with the silent men.

I can see *Ludzas iela* ahead!

It is different now. Divided right down the middle by high barbed wire and posts with warning notices pinned to them.

As I am straining to try and see where we are going I jostle the man next to me and he knocks my cap off.

It falls to the ground as if in slow motion.

I make a grab at my hair with one hand and hold it up while I fumble on the ground for the cap but it is too late. For one flash, my long brown hair has tumbled around my shoulders and down my back and the man next to me has seen.

He bends down and picks up the cap. He hands it back to me and for the first time I see his face clearly in the moonlight.

It's a young man, more of a boy. Sharp-featured, with fair hair that falls over one side of his face and the pale grey sheen of un-nourished skin that we all have.

I don't know who's more shocked.

I can't speak but I implore the boy with my eyes as hard as I can.

Don't tell them. Please.

The boy recovers himself fast. He moves in front of me a little to shield me with his body and with a brief jerk of his head, signals me to put my cap back on.

I shove it on with a shaking hand and push my lank mass of hair up inside it.

God has answered my prayers for the second time today.

Chapter Twenty-one

I WOULD LIKE TO THANK this boy, but I can't.

The SS have stripped us Jews of all rights, including being able to talk when we want to. I swallow down great painful lumps of relief.

The boy risks a low whisper.

"I thought all the children were dead," he says. "We heard rumours."

I give a small shake of my head and offer a tiny smile. More of a cheek-twitch, really, but then there's a policeman about a metre ahead of us and he's armed.

"I am the only one who survived the forest," I say, my whisper cracking as I realize the truth of what I'm saying.

We have reached the gates of the Small Ghetto now

and random men are being checked. I swallow. One more removal of my cap and the game is up for me.

I shuffle by. The boy tries to block me from view a little and it works.

No checks for me today.

I am back in the grounds of the Small Ghetto.

I have no idea where I am supposed to go for the night.

"Do you know a boy called Max?" I mutter, as low as I can. "I need to find him. Or can I get a message to him through you?"

"There is a women's block now," the boy hisses. "68 *Ludzas*. Go there. Tomorrow our work detail leaves from the usual place. If you can get a note to me I will try and find him."

I nod, tears rising up. I am not used to kindness from strangers any more.

Then I walk down *Ludzas iela* to try and find my new home.

The women's block is on the opposite side of the street to the apartment at number 29 where I used to live with Mama and Omama. That half of the street remains in the Large Ghetto but seems deserted. The half that I am in now houses the remainder of the Small Ghetto inhabitants.

The building I stop in front of is five storeys high and made of a dirty, yellow-grey concrete.

I take off my cap, careful that no guard is watching me.

I shake my dirty hair free and let it fall around my shoulders.

Then I take a weary breath and head inside.

Upstairs there are lots of rooms with doors wide open.

I am so tired and dizzy and traumatized that I just walk into the first one that I find.

There are women lying in groups all over the floor.

At least – I think they are women.

Some of them are so thin and ill-looking that at first I can't tell what sex they are at all.

Others are still able to stand and are leaning up against the walls or looking out of the window in a desultory way, like they don't really expect to see anything out of it.

One of these women sees me standing in a daze in the doorway and comes over just in time for me to fall half on top of her.

"Steady," she says. She supports me into the room and lowers me down with care onto a holey mattress. She has long chestnut-coloured hair streaked with grey. Her face is very thin and she's wearing a shapeless coat and a dark scarf wrapped half over her face.

"Where have you come from?" she says. "We all arrived here yesterday."

I seem to not be able to speak.

It all comes back in a wash of horror.

The pit – Mama, falling into it on her knees. Sascha tumbling after her. The cries and moans coming from the red earth.

The warmth of Mama's back against my skin.

I bury my face on my knees and begin to rock from side to side.

It takes me several hours to be able to speak.

I just sit and rock and shake in the corner of the room.

The woman, whose name I find out is Lina, makes me a cup of weak black coffee. The drink scalds and burns my stomach but it feels good to have something warm.

I can't stop shaking. Every time I close my eyes I see the forest again and Mama being shot and my body is wracked with spasms.

Lina sits next to me on the mattress and holds my hand with her thin one.

"We all came back yesterday," she says, gesturing at the

other women. "We were being held in the Central Prison because we are good seamstresses. Apparently we are going to get work for the German army soon."

I stare at her in disbelief. My head computes like mad.

So these are the women who were in the prison with Mama and me.

These are the women who turned right instead of left.

The ones we thought were going to die.

Aren't you just the daughters of fortune?

These are the women that the guard in the prison was referring to. Now I understand.

He knew what was happening to the rest of the Jews of Rīga. He knew that these few women would be given a chance to survive.

Mama and I joined the wrong queue. We thought that if we came back to the ghetto earlier we would be safe.

We got it the wrong way round.

That split-second decision has resulted in her death.

I begin to cry again.

That night I recover my voice.

In a whisper I tell the women about the massacre in the Rumbula forest.

There are cries and shrieks as I describe it. Some of the

women faint. They were hoping against hope that their relatives might after all have been "resettled" in an actual work camp elsewhere.

"We suspected, of course," says Lina. "We knew about the first 'resettlement' and we saw on the way back here all the empty buildings in the Large Ghetto and the unfinished meals on the tables. Nobody lives there now. There are just the few of us left in the Small Ghetto and we will have to go to work soon. But we always had hope."

"Oh," I say in a tiny whisper. "I did not want to take away your hope."

Lina hugs me.

"It's okay," she says. "I think we already knew, deep down."

She is pensive, gazing at her feet in their grey lace-up leather shoes with holes all along the side.

It occurs to me with a stabbing pain that nearly all these women sitting here on their own have lost somebody in the forest too.

So these are the sole survivors of the Jewish women of Rīga. Lina tells me that there are about three hundred of us crammed into this one building.

There are no words.

Somebody has got hold of a candle and somebody else has a precious hidden supply of matches.

A handful of the women mutter the Kaddish, our Jewish Prayer for the Dead.

We sit up for most of the night and watch the flame in silence.

The next morning we are woken early by a commotion on the other side of the fence.

On the half of the street which is now off limits to us residents of the Small Ghetto, a long column of people clutching small bags is being marched in.

The people all have a bewildered look on their faces. They are walking in silence, looking up at the ramshackle buildings with fear in their eyes.

They are not from Rīga, I am sure of it. Something about their clothes and their skin and the way they are looking around makes me think that they are from somewhere different.

"Oh my God," says Lina. She is watching next to me, clutching a cup to her chest and inhaling the warm steam as it rises. We have one pokey, greasy little kitchen where we can use a tap. "They are bringing foreign Jews into the Large Ghetto."

We watch in silence as the bewildered mass of people start to enter the abandoned buildings of the Large Ghetto.

What sights must await them. There are breakfasts still abandoned on tables, children's toys strewn over the floor, cupboards open, blood smeared on the walls, maybe even the remains of people left for dead.

"My God," says Lina again, quieter this time.

"That is why they killed them. So they could move Jews from other countries in."

"Don't be silly," says another woman from behind us in the room. She is older, with grey hair in a tight bun and crow's feet around her blue eyes. "Even the SS would not do that, surely?"

Her comment is greeted with total silence.

The weight of what we are starting to understand threatens to push us all down into oblivion.

We are expected to start work the next morning.

I am disappointed. I want to go and find Max so much. I need to see his kind dark eyes and know that I still have my friend. But Lina tells me that we are strictly forbidden to mix with the men of the Small Ghetto even though they are only a few buildings away and there will be no time to find him. I realize that my only hope is to find the kind boy who helped me last night and get him to take a note. So I persuade one of the women to give me a piece of her precious paper supply and I borrow a pencil from one of the other women. I write him a note. This is what I write:

Need to see you. I have sad news of Sascha. She died with Mama in the forest. We looked after her until then and we were with her right until the end. I think she knew that we loved her. I am so sorry to have to tell you this. I hope you are okay and that you have found your father.

I don't sign it. Signing my name to anything would be like asking for an instant death sentence.

He will know who it is from.

Then I shove it in my pocket as we are shouted outside into the streets and formed into columns. I am wearing the women's clothing that I took from the Rumbula forest.

The men and the women's columns leave from different parts of the Small Ghetto but they merge together once we are on *Maskavas iela* and heading into town.

I notice that some of the other women are casting glances at the men. Some of them still have husbands and sons alive here. It must be torture for them not to be able to speak, or touch, or spend any time together.

I inch my way along our column, bit by bit so that I don't attract the attention of the guards. I strain my eyes in case I see Max but as many of the men are wearing the same dark caps and coats it is difficult.

Then a pale oval face half-turns towards where I'm standing and I see the boy who saved me. He has been looking out for me.

I position myself in the women's column again and shuffle along until I am right by him. With a lightning manoeuvre I shove the scrap of paper into his pocket and then fade back into line again. My heart thuds. Nobody seems to have noticed.

The men turn off towards the factories in town and we are marched on further. I have no idea where we are going but we are sent on for another half-hour's tedious cold walk in the ice and snow and in the end we come to an old market hall on the far side of the old town.

Inside the hall are vast piles of clothing, heaped up towards the ceiling.

Lina gasps when she sees them. She clutches my arm for support.

"Please God don't let these be what I think," she says.

I have been praying the same.

Inside we are placed at long tables and for the whole day we sort belongings into piles. We separate coats and jackets from dresses and trousers. If we find any valuables in the pockets we put them in a box under the table. We are commanded to cut the yellow stars off all the coats and jackets and put them in a separate box underneath the table.

The work is not difficult but it is relentless.

I sort coats from jackets and remove yellow stars with a snip of scissors or sometimes they are so loose I can pull the cotton off with my hands.

I start to notice little details as I pick up shirts and blouses and sort them into piles.

Many of the clothes have holes in. The holes are big enough for me to put my finger through. Sometimes they are bordered with something dark red, almost black.

Many of the clothes are tiny. Little white dresses, miniature pairs of grey flannel trousers. Pink baby bonnets and tiny brown caps.

It's like my brain shuts down at this point.

I go into a mechanical state, like a doll in a museum.

I sort. If I find a necklace or a tiny jewel I throw it into the box underneath my legs.

I do this for eight hours and manage to keep my eyes clear of tears and my heart thudding in a dull fashion underneath my clothes.

And then I see it.

I would recognize it anywhere. It has Mama's neat stitching all round the hem. She complained when she was doing it, but with the smile that meant she didn't mind.

"I don't have black cotton or even any brown so you will have to put up with red," she said.

“Good God in Heaven, I will look as if I belong to the travelling circus,” said Omama.

And that’s how I distinguish my grandmother’s winter coat from all the other black coats that sit in heaps around me.

I push my finger through the hole in the chest. It is just below the yellow star. My finger wiggles, pink and alive against the dull rust stains surrounding the hole.

Without even stopping to check where the guards are, I pull off the star with a shaking hand and slip it into my pocket.

The tears run in silence down my cheeks.

Our food is running low.

We have managed to find out that there is a secret bakery operating in our building in the back room on the ground floor. There a woman is baking matzo for the Sabbath. The Nazis have retained a small number of the Jewish Police to keep us in order but the policewoman who guards our block has turned a blind eye to the baking and it is rumoured that she is the one who smuggles in flour.

So we have matzo once a week to supplement the rations from the store but it is not enough to give us strength to work in the way that we have to.

And then in the harsh depths of winter, I get sick.

If you are too sick to work, you either go to the hospital in the Small Ghetto and risk catching something worse from the other patients, or you are "resettled" out of the camp, or you are shot where you lie in bed in your ghetto room.

Some choice.

At first I carry on dragging myself across town in the column every morning to get to work. I have been transferred with most of the other women to a sewing workshop near the river where we repair the uniforms of the German army.

Lina holds me up by the arm on the long walk to work. She has got a lot quieter. I know that she found the clothing belonging to her children when she worked at the sorting depot. She came home that day and collapsed. Since then we have tried to support one another. So Lina tries to make it look as if I am walking to work but really she is half-carrying, half-pushing me.

When we get to our workplace I bend my head over a sewing machine and mend the tough green fabrics of German army uniforms. I try to hold in my cough but it's not easy. My shoulders shake and my chest feels like it's going to burst. The cough only stops when I swallow down the weak black coffee that we are given at lunchtime.

One morning I wake up on the floor in my corner of the women's block with the usual pains in my bones from the hard mattress and the usual pangs of hunger gnawing away beneath my sharp rib-bones and as usual I have been bitten by lice all through the night so my body is a mass of hard, swollen red lumps which itch like hell, and I realize that on top of this I am sweating and hot.

I lie still on my mattress, shivering under the rotten fabric which passes as a blanket.

I put my hand on my forehead. It is burning hot, so hot that I snatch my hand away in a panic.

"Lina," I call. Lina comes over from the other side of the room where she is saying her prayers. She says them every morning before work. I see her clutch a red ribbon which belonged to her little daughter.

"My head is burning up," I say. "And everything has gone swimmy."

Lina does the same as me, laying her thin hand on my hot head. Tears prick my eyes. She does it like Mama would have done.

Lina frowns.

"I think you will have to go to the hospital block," she says. "This doesn't look too good, Hanna."

I feel sick with panic. The room swirls about and closes in on me.

"But I have to try and keep going," I say. "I promised Papa."

Lina gives me a gentle hug. We are all thin enough to snap.

"I will be able to visit you," she says. "They allow visits. It will be all right."

She helps me get dressed. The feeling of the cloth on my skin burns but I have to wear something as it is still freezing outside. Lina half-carries me down the stairs and around the corner to the small hospital block. I am hardly aware of what we are doing. The fever is making me moan and wince in pain.

I am received into the hospital and put on a ward into a clean white bed. It is like being in Heaven. It is a long time since I slept in a proper bed.

"Don't worry," says the only Jewish doctor left. "We will look after her. You should keep away. She may have typhus."

My heart contracts when he says this.

I think: *No. First Papa is taken away, then Omama dies and then Mama. It is not my time. I have to keep going.*

But these feelings are overtaken by a burning fever.

I lose awareness of everything.

*

For three days I am delirious with a high temperature and a wracking cough.

The staff shave all my hair off. Something to do with stopping the spread of typhus.

I wake up from my fever feeling light and strange.

My head on the pillow is cold even though the rest of my body is warm.

I raise my hand to my head and feel only a cold shiny dome of skin.

I scream.

Lina is there and tries to calm me down.

"You have been very sick," she says. "They had to do it. There has been such an epidemic of typhus."

I hold her bony hand in mine.

"Why are you here, then?" I say. "Surely you don't want to catch it too?"

Lina shrugs.

"If I do, I do," she says. "There is nothing left for me outside, even if we do escape this blessed place in the end. Nobody left."

She looks so tired and sad that I can't speak for a moment.

This is what has become of us.

*

But there is hope for me.

Somewhere out there I am convinced that my papa is still alive. I do not know how I know this. I just feel it. I have always felt it.

And there is more. Lina brings in a visitor.

"Oh!" I say. I struggle into a sitting position and try to adjust my hair before I realize I don't have any now.

"I must look so bad," I say. "Sorry."

Max sits by my bed.

He has got very thin. I can see the skull under his eye sockets and there are pale veins bulging out of his neck.

"I did not think I would ever see you again," I say. I am grinning like a lunatic. It is so good to have both these dear faces by my bedside. For a moment I feel as if I am not totally alone.

"I got your note," says Max. "Plus my father is working in the hospital kitchen. He is making the revolting soup that you will be offered later."

"Oh," I say. Relief and jealousy flood over me in equal measures. Max has been reunited with Janis. Together they still count as a family.

I gaze up into Max's warm brown eyes. I could stare at his face all day.

I realize something at that moment. Max is kind, deep down where it really matters. He is as different to Uldis as hot chocolate is to a bottle of Rīga Black Balsam.

Lina smiles and fades into the background.

Max holds my hand.

"I am sorry about your grandmother and mother," he says in a hesitant voice. "They were good to me. Good people."

I nod. For a moment I can't speak. Then I remember.

"And I am so sorry about Sascha and having to tell you in a note," I say. "But I thought I might not get to see you in the flesh again."

Max's eyes fill with pain.

"What sort of world is this?" he says. "Where little children are shot like rabbits."

The anger in his voice frightens me.

"We will get out of here soon," I say. "When I am better I will come and find you. There must be a way."

Max gives a dry laugh. It is not a sound of amusement.

"Yeah," he says, standing and putting his cap back on. "But I don't think we Jews will be allowed to use it."

Then he gives me a quick kiss on the forehead and leaves.

I can feel the imprint of that kiss for days.

*

I never get to leave the hospital of my own accord.

On the fifth day just as I am feeling stronger and better than I have for a while, thanks to the soup and bread I am given twice a day, a commotion starts up outside.

The nurse in charge of my ward wanders over to the window and peers out.

Her body stiffens.

"SS!" she yells down the corridor to the nursing station.

The nurses start to scurry up and down the wards. They tell us all to lie down and look as sick and germ-ridden as possible. They encourage us to cough because the Nazis are fearful of all disease.

I pull the sheet up to my head, shaking. With my bald head I imagine I look like a giant white egg lying on a striped pillow.

There are trucks and SS vehicles outside.

I can hear the dogs.

Footsteps pound into the entrance area of the hospital and then members of the SS burst into our ward and stare at us.

They go out again and begin to bark out orders.

A nurse comes to my bedside, pale with fright. I can see that she is trying to appear calm for my sake.

"Put this on," she says. She is holding my dress and coat out.

I stand on the cold hard floor of the ward. My legs feel like icicles that might snap at any moment. I let her help me with the dress and coat and then I put my boots back on. My feet are so thin now that the boots feel heavy and too big.

I am helped out of the ward along with all the other patients. Some of them are very old and still very sick. The nurses try to support them as much as they can.

A male doctor hovers behind us, watching the SS as they order everybody outside.

"I beg you to be compassionate," he calls. "These are my patients. They are to be treated with care."

An SS man laughs in his face.

"They are Jews," he says. "They will get what is coming to them."

The SS in their dark green uniforms pace up and down by the trucks, their dogs snarling and barking in the direction of the hospital. Some of the men now wear thick long leather coats to protect them against the winter cold.

They wear these coats while we sleep at night on bare boards with glassless windows. Our clothes have holes in and our boots let in the water.

These thoughts pass through my head in a mess. Along with a stream of old women and younger women in white hospital gowns I am being herded up the front path of the hospital and towards the waiting trucks.

Nurses and doctors in uniform are being hustled along with us. There is so much shouting and chaos that at first I can't make out what is going on.

But then I see her.

Lina.

Running from the direction of the women's block towards the hospital as fast as her thin legs can manage.

"Hanna!" she screams. "Hold on. I'm coming."

"Quick!" shouts an SS man from behind me. He pushes me in the back with his gun and I stumble onto the path, landing on my wrists.

"No!" screams Lina. "You can't take her. Leave her with me! I will look after her."

She has reached the gate to the hospital but is being held back by a line of SS men with guns.

I stand up again, dizzy, but my knees give way.

I am no fool.

I know why a truckload of old and sick people is being taken from the hospital.

And the only person who can save me is being hit around the face by an SS man with a gun and a black snarling red-eyed dog.

"Lina," I say, but my voice has deserted me. All that comes out is a cracked whisper.

I am pushed up into the back of the truck and land on the hard floor in a tangle of sore bones.

There is a gunshot somewhere behind me and a scream.

My heart runs cold.

The engine roars into life.

I don't look back.

Chapter Twenty-two

We are not in the truck for long.

Most of the patients lie on the floor, moaning and crying. Some of them are no more than heaps of joined-up bones clad in white rags.

I sit with my back against the wall of the vehicle. I am shaking with cold and my stomach aches. I am still weak from the typhus.

There is nobody here for me now.

I think of Max's kind face and my heart threatens to split in two.

If only I could have let him know what was happening.

He will find out soon enough.

But there is nothing he can do.

*

I take my first proper look at the other passengers in the back of the truck.

Some of them are very old, their faces creased with wisdom and angst, expressions of complete passivity and resignation sketched over their features. There are younger women with their arms in slings and their bodies covered in sores and bandages. They wear the same expressions as the older women.

Only the nurses and female doctors who have been thrown in with us look frightened, but they are already starting to try and tend to the sicker patients, redoing bandages, offering mouthfuls of bread hidden in pockets and sips of water from concealed flasks.

We are pushed off the truck at the train station near to the Central Prison.

I see the needle-shaped turrets rising up towards the empty winter sky and I think how long ago it seems that Mama and I were in there. Back then we had humour and each other and a little physical strength. We had enough hope to think that we were going to survive.

Now we are rounded up by barking dogs and pushed up into a dirty brown train which does not look like it is supposed to transport people. We are hounded up ramps and beaten into dark sealed cars.

Over one hundred women are shoved into this one car.

They cry out as their bones hit the floor. There is some sort of rough sawdust on the floor and a strong smell of human excrement mixed with a fainter smell of animal.

I realize that the trucks have been used for transporting cattle.

So that is what we have become.

No better than herds of farm animals. But at least the animals get to spend time outside in the fields. At least they are fed and can feel the warmth of the sun on their backs in summer.

This is what happened to Papa. He was shoved into one of these trucks and taken God only knows where. He might have been starving just like us.

He might have been shot dead.

But I refuse to believe that last bit.

I find a spot and sit down in the corner of the carriage next to a rusting iron bucket.

The bucket is full of faeces and urine. It stinks. There is a small hole in the floor of the carriage so I try to pour as much as I can down onto the tracks but it is so heavy that much of the contents slop over the floor instead and a woman snaps at me to leave it.

More and more women are shoved in on top of me. Compared to this, our room in the women's block was paradise. I have somebody's elbow in my face and somebody else's legs across my own, which stick out on the floor in front of me.

It is so dark and claustrophobic in here that I cannot even see who these people are.

All I hear is moaning and wailing and muttering and voices calling out in panic through the one tiny window high up on the side of the car. The window is covered in barbed wire.

Nobody comes.

The train sits there for what feels like ages.

Then with a great grinding jolt it begins to move. Through the tiny window I can just make out the figure of an armed guard standing on the step outside the next carriage.

The women scream as they are thrown on top of others with injuries and propelled forwards with the motion of the train.

"Where are we going?" I say, to anyone who might be listening. I can't see very clearly as it is so dark in here. "What are the bastards doing to us now?"

I sound like Omama. My eyes fill with tears.

Nobody replies.

I grip my own hand in the darkness.

The train rattles on, neither slow nor fast but at some

indeterminate speed heading towards some indeterminate location.

It becomes colder in the car despite the hundreds of bodies crammed inside.

Flurries of snow start to wend their way through the small barbed-wire window at the top of the car.

Women sigh with pain as they relieve themselves onto the floor of the carriage and then cry with shame when they realize the stench and mess are not going to go anywhere.

I try to sit on the bucket but I am too weak to squat in one position and the contents slop over the side and all over my feet.

I take off my coat and try to mop myself up as best I can. I want to put the coat back on because I only have one thin pullover underneath and the air coming through the tiny window is freezing but my coat is now soaked in urine. In the end I put it on anyway. I sit huddled in it, holding on to my own elbows and try to warm my arms that way.

As the train grinds on some women fall asleep sitting up and others cry or pray.

"Water," they beg every time the train appears to stop at a station.

Nobody brings any.

One or two people have managed to smuggle out bits of paper and stubs of pencil. They scribble notes on the paper and push the fragments through the hole in the floor onto the tracks below.

"What good will that do?" complain others. "Who is going to see them?"

I think I understand. It is giving those women who wrote the notes a last glimmer of hope.

We travel on.

I lean against the side of the carriage and am surprised to realize that I don't mind being a Jew any longer. I have learned something on my journey. I have learned that the only people worth knowing are the ones who accept me for who I am and not what I am. Mama, Papa, Omama, Max, Lina, Uncle Georgs.

I wonder if the people lying in heaps around me have realized this. It seems very important that they should hear my revelation, but I feel too weak to open my mouth to ask anybody.

I doze for a bit.

When I wake up Mama is sitting next to me.

I think I might be dying. I have heard about the last hallucinations witnessed by people who are soon to leave this earth.

She is sitting next to me and smiling. Her hair has

become lush and brown again and she is all fleshed out with health.

"Sing, Hanna," she says. "You have such a lovely voice."

I clear my throat. It is dark in here and nobody can really see me. I still feel a little shy, though.

I think. Then I decide to sing the Hativka. It is our Jewish anthem.

At first my voice wavers, particularly when everybody else in the car shuts up to listen. Then I find strength from somewhere inside. My voice rises, pure and clear. A few people join in, their voices disjointed and weak, but it is like they are clinging to a life raft for those few moments.

When I have finished Mama squeezes my hand.

"Still Papa's little songbird," she whispers.

Then she fades away.

Our journey in the hell of that carriage continues through a night and into another day.

I do not feel much now. No anger, no fear, not even pain. I am just numb all over, in my head and in my limbs. I think my soul has already left my body and flown off somewhere warm, leaving a jumble of bones behind on the filthy carriage floor.

I watch a mixture of snow and sunshine through the high window. The barbed wire makes diamond patterns in the sky. It is quite pretty, although the scene in our carriage is anything but.

Then something happens.

A woman who until now has been sitting next to us, and muttering to herself in an agitated tone, stands up.

With frenetic gestures and an unexpected brute strength she tears at the barbed wire across the window with her bare hands and manages to rip the central section apart.

Then she begins to climb on top of me so that she can push her head out of the window.

"Ow!" I scream, trying to get her boot out of my face. "Get off me!"

Another woman starts to swear.

"How dare you crush a child!" she says. "If you need to stand on somebody, use me."

The woman is trying to push herself head-first through the window. She gets her head and shoulders through but she has not accounted for the armed Latvian police who stand outside the carriages at all times of day and night.

There's a shout. A shot.

The woman's legs go limp.

They hang down on top of us where we sit.

"Dear God," says the woman who stood up for me.

"We will have to pull her in again."

With the help of another woman we pull the corpse back inside. It flops down next to me and I try to shuffle away a little but there is no room.

My fingers touch something sticky on the floor. There is nothing I can do. We have no cloths, no water, no space.

For hours I sit next to the body of the woman.

I look up at the broken barbed-wire window.

"The snow is much heavier," Mama whispers in my ear. "And the train is slowing down. Perfect."

"You're back!" I say. I don't care whether I am dreaming or hallucinating. I am sure I can hear my mother's voice in my ear.

Great thick flakes are now falling fast outside.

"You are thin enough, Hanna," she says.

For a moment I am confused. I know I am thin. Why is she telling me? I can feel what used to be my buttocks and are now two big bones pressing into the hard floor of the train.

Mama takes my face in her hands. There is no warmth in her skin but I feel comforted.

"Go," she says. "You have a chance. I will help you."

I glance around. Maybe I am finally losing my mind. I have heard that it happens to people who are very sick.

"Go where, Mama?" I say. "We haven't arrived yet."

My mother's profile in the dim light is tilted up towards the window.

With a pang of true horror I realize what she is suggesting.

"No way," I say. "I would never get through that window. Anyway, I am not leaving you and that is final. I promised Papa."

Mama traces the tears on my cheeks with her finger. There is something heavy upon my head. I realize with a dull twang that my hair has somehow come back again. She strokes my plait like she did when I was little. I have a dirty piece of string holding the ends together now, instead of a red ribbon.

"If you get out of here you may get to see Papa again one day," she whispers. "I would like that."

"But you have to come with us," I say. I am crying now. "We're not a family without you."

Mama sighs.

"Hanna," she says. "I have already gone. You have your whole life ahead. Somebody has to tell the world what has happened to us Jews. You could tell the truth."

I am shaking now. With tears, with fright and with the enormity of what I am about to do.

"Mama…" I begin.

But my mother gestures at me to stand on top of the dead woman.

Most of the women in the carriage are asleep, but I sense some of them watching me with dull, disinterested eyes.

Most of them have given up on life.

But I, Hanna Michelson, the ballerina from Rīga?

I have the strangest feeling. There is a tiny stirring of something resembling my old spirit, deep within my starved, wrecked body.

I realize something. It gives me a real jolt of surprise.

I want to get old!

I want to get cranky and bent over and wrinkled, like Omama.

I have decided!

Mama was right. The snow is much heavier now.

I stretch up and place my hands on the bottom of the gaping barbed-wire window. The broken wire cuts my hands but I no longer feel pain in the way that I used to.

I pull some of the strands of wire aside.

"I am coming, Papa," I say out loud, like a crazy lady.

"Should I push you up?" says the woman who helped me before. "I've got nothing to lose."

I feel a flash of pure panic.

"I can't do this," I say.

"You could try," says the woman. "You're very thin and small. You will need to go legs first. When you get out jump quick, before the guard sees you."

A second woman agrees to help. They ignore the moans and cries of protest from all the other people who are lying near to us and have to shuffle themselves out of the way.

I feel two sets of bony arms, pushing and heaving me up towards the tiny window until my legs hit the freezing air. The arms push me through the small gap as if they are posting a large parcel through a small letter box. My coat gets caught on the wire and I struggle to move forwards, but then I remember my ballet training. I let my body go as loose and flexible as I can and the women below keep pushing me until most of my body has scraped over the broken wire and is hanging outside the carriage. I grip the sill of the window with my frozen hands and hang on.

Only my head remains inside the carriage.

"Remember to tell our story," says the first woman. "You can make sure that people know."

I look down. I can't see Mama.

My tears drip into the dark carriage below.

"God bless," Mama whispers, from somewhere far away.

And then I am out.

*

I am standing on the ridge that covers one of the train's wheels.

My head is in a blur of snow and cold and dark and for a moment I feel as if I am just going to fall under the wheels of the train.

I grip the side of the carriage. The wooden slats are thick with ice. My hands keep slipping off. I put them back up over the edge of the broken window and hold on to that instead.

The snow is thick, but not thick enough to hide the sight of an armed guard standing on the step outside the next carriage along.

He is carrying a long rifle and wearing a fur hat and long shiny boots.

He is facing towards me.

Everything seems to slow down.

I freeze. I cannot jump. My legs have turned to pulp.

The man raises his rifle with a deliberate action and points it at my head.

The snow lessens a little and I see his face.

My heart jolts with shock.

I know those eyes.

Cold, blue, set into a sharp, chiselled face.

I don't think he recognizes me.

"Uldis!" I shout against the noise of the train. "It is me. Hanna. Don't shoot!"

My voice is too thin to pierce the muted white wilderness swirling around us.

There is a moment where everything seems to stop.

I am no longer aware of the biting cold on my fingers where they still grip the train.

I don't see the flakes circling around my head or feel the chill in my feet.

I focus with the greatest concentration I have ever had in my life. I am trying to get the thoughts to travel from my head to where he is standing.

I stare straight at him and block out the world until it shrinks down to him and me on the outside of a cattle truck travelling to a death camp and I think:

For every time you sat around the table with us.

For the times we used to go to the cinema and I wanted to hold your hand but was too shy.

For all those times my mama gave you her best food and my omama pinched your cheek so hard it hurt.

For all the times you sat and discussed your future with my papa and he gave you advice.

For everything I ever felt for you, Uldis. For everything you might have felt for me if I wasn't a dirty Jew.

I know that there is still a good part of you.

Please.

I stare at the round end of the gun's muzzle. It is lined up with my forehead. I try to imagine what the bullet will feel like.

Our eyes lock.

The world stops moving. It is the longest minute a person could ever know.

Please.

The gun is lowered. With a slow, deliberate gesture he turns his head in the opposite direction.

That's when I do it.

I jump.

The snow receives me like a glove.

Afterword

AFTER THE MAJORITY OF THE Jews from Rīga were killed, the Large Ghetto became known instead as the German Ghetto and the Nazis arranged for huge numbers of German Jews to be moved in. Periodic killings continued, although not on the scale of the Rumbula murders. In November 1943, a train containing around 2,000 sick and elderly people from the ghetto, among them children, was sent to Auschwitz where all perished in the gas chambers.

At the end of November 1943, the Rīga Ghetto was finally closed down. Rīga Ghetto prisoners who were unable to work elsewhere were brought to the Biķernieki forest near Rīga and murdered. In 1944 the few surviving Jews from Rīga along with Jews from other parts of Europe still capable of working were sent to the Kaiserwald Concentration Camp on the outskirts of the city. Those unable to work at Kaiserwald were murdered during 1944 at the Biķernieki forest. This forest became known as Latvia's biggest mass murder site of the Holocaust during the years 1941–44. About 46,500 people were reported to have been killed there, including Latvian and Western European Jews, Soviet prisoners of war, and the Nazis' political adversaries.

There were only three known survivors of the Rumbula forest massacres, who later gave accounts: Frida Michelson, Elle Madale, and Matiss Lutrins. Michelson survived by pretending to be dead, as victims discarded heaps of shoes on her. Madale claimed to be a Latvian. Lutrins persuaded some Latvian truck drivers to allow him and his wife (whom the Nazis later found and killed) to hide under clothing from the victims that was being taken back to Rīga.

As Stalin's Red Army advanced again on Latvia in August 1944, the Nazis began to evacuate inmates from Kaiserwald to Stutthof Concentration Camp in Poland. Conditions there were appalling and many died.

After Rīga was reoccupied by the Soviets, a notebook lay in an empty school building in which any surviving Jews could sign their name. Only 150 names were recorded in that book, which is now held at the United States Holocaust Memorial Museum.

Rīga was ruled by a Communist government right up until 1991, when Latvia finally regained independence – the first time they had done so since 1920.

About the Author

VANESSA CURTIS is an award-winning author of books for teens and children, including *Zelah Green* which won the Manchester Children's Book Prize and was shortlisted for the Waterstones Children's Book Prize, and *The Earth is Singing*, winner of the Young Quills Historical Association Award, shortlisted for Peters Books of the Year Award and longlisted for the Carnegie Medal.

She is also one of the co-founders of The Virginia Woolf Society of Great Britain and the author of two biographies on Virginia Woolf. Vanessa reviews books for national newspapers and runs The Curtis Children's Literary Consultancy, specialising in YA fiction.

Usborne Quicklinks

For links to websites where you can take a virtual tour of the Rīga Ghetto, find information about the Holocaust, Nazi Germany and the Second World War, and discover more about Judaism, go to the Usborne Quicklinks website at www.usborne.com/quicklinks and enter the keywords "The Earth is Singing". Please follow the online safety guidelines at the Usborne Quicklinks website.

Discussion Questions

- When the German army arrives in Rīga they are welcomed by the Latvians and Hanna is hopeful that *"they will make things better"*. Why do you think this is?

- Mama and Omama are aware of the potential dangers they face when Latvia is occupied by the Nazis. Discuss their decision to stay.

- In Chapter Six, Hanna says, "*I don't want to be Jewish. I am going to be Latvian and not Jewish from now on. I will not wear the star.*" Consider your response to Hanna's outburst, and the effects of wearing the star.

- Imagine you are being forced to leave your home and can only pack what you can carry. What would you take, and why?

- "*Prayer is free*," says Omama. "*We can have as much of that as we want. The Nazis can't take that away from us.*" Throughout the book, the Michelsons continue to practise the Jewish faith and observe Jewish rituals. Why do you think they do this?

- Do you believe Uldis ever cared for Hanna? Why do you think he betrays the Michelsons to the Nazis?

- Does everybody obey the Nazis all the time? What acts of resistance, small and large, can you find in the book?

- "*We are like animals trapped in the zoo.*" In Chapter Fourteen we learn there are 30,000 people crammed into sixteen blocks in the ghetto. What impact do you think living in these conditions had on people, and on how those outside the ghetto perceived them?

- What are your thoughts on the book's title?

- Throughout the book, Hanna remains focused on surviving in order to tell her story. Why is this so important?